"I wish you had gone back the way you came."

Danielle's voice was reproachful as she continued, "When you found me asleep, you should have left."

"Wasting a time and a place that took all my audacity to contrive?" Cabot asked huskily.

"You had to make use of some luck, too," she pointed out.

"In finding you available without having to keep my foot in the door? Surely," Cabot agreed, adding, "My star was in the ascendant." He stood looking down at her where she lay on the bed. "But now that we're both here, mightn't we try putting some zing into our relationship? We have a right to get some enjoyment out of its necessity. How much practice in enjoying each other have we had? None at all!"

JANE ARBOR
is also the author of these
Harlequin Romances

Many of these books are available at your local bookseller.

For a free catalog listing all titles currently available,
send your name and address to:

HARLEQUIN READER SERVICE
1440 South Priest Drive, Tempe, AZ 85281
Canadian address: Stratford, Ontario N5A 6W2

Handmaid to Midas

Jane Arbor

Harlequin Books

TORONTO • NEW YORK • LOS ANGELES • LONDON
AMSTERDAM • PARIS • SYDNEY • HAMBURG
STOCKHOLM • ATHENS • TOKYO • MILAN

Original hardcover edition published in 1982
by Mills & Boon Limited

ISBN 0-373-02545-9

Harlequin Romance first edition May 1983

CHAPTER ONE

BLACK glass and chromium, an elevator so swift that it left your stomach to follow you, upper corridors which gave a near-aerial view of the city, and an outer office with the floor-area of a throne-room.

'I might have guessed,' was Danielle's mental flashback to the humble Georgian terrace in south London which, by ruling of the majesty reigning here, was home to her no longer.

Behind a mahogany desk a sylph came to her feet and motioned Danielle to a chair. In a flat Mayfair accent she said, 'Miss Kane? Mr Steele knows you're here and will ring when he's ready to see you—Ah, there's his bell now. Yes, that door——' She deigned to cross the floor to open it for Danielle, who went through it to more mahogany and glass, though in a smaller setting.

The man who rose and extended a hand across his desk was no stranger to her either by sight or reputation. Anyone who followed the media would recognise at a glance Cabot Steele, property developer, and anyone who had been or knew a victim of his would have to acknowledge that the man's stature and looks carried the hallmark of his power.

He towered. Above narrow athletic hips his torso was lean and controlled, his shoulders wide. His face was darkly saturnine, strong of nose and haggard beyond his reputed late-thirties age. Strength of character, or a stubbornly dominant will passing for character, must have drawn every line of his features. There was an occasional tawny glint in his deep-set eyes, and his thick auburn hair, smoothly brushed back, subscribed to no particular male fashion. In his perfectly tailored city clothes he was as splendidly sleek and assured as a newly groomed tiger—with the tiger's claws which Danielle longed to blunt well sheathed for the moment.

She hadn't known the source of the oddly worded advertisement when she had replied to it to a solicitors' office in Norfolk Street. Stating, *Required—Friday person for temporary service in private yacht presently visiting Mediterranean ports,* it had whetted her curiosity, puzzling her until the reference dawned on her. Some wealthy eccentric going cruising needed a yes-man, an all-duties factotum whom he would whimsically call his Man Friday and demand his attentions all the hours there were. She had pitied the poor chap, dismissing the advertisement as not for her. And yet— 'Friday *person*?' That meant someone of either sex, and temporary service of this kind or that was her business. A Mediterranean cruise was inviting and, however exacting the role, the job couldn't last for ever. Besides, she needed the money. It had been worth the price of a postage stamp to reply.

This morning she had walked up Norfolk Street into The Strand, still fingering the piece of engraved pasteboard she had been given at the office. Summoned by telephone to wait on their client at noon, she had been presented with his card by the solicitors' clerk and had been politely ushered on her way almost before she had read the name of Cabot Steele on the card and had admitted that yes, she knew the Steele building well.

In the Strand she hadn't given herself time to question the strange chance her fate had dealt her. She had hailed the first taxi that came along, and here she was now, face to face with the man who she knew wouldn't recognise her for one of the many puny, impotent enemies he had made for himself along his ruthless way.

She took his proffered hand briefly and sat down at his gesture. He remained standing himself, then came round his desk, propping his long thighs against it, and studying her.

It was a penetrating scrutiny, as unnecessary as it was embarrassing, she felt. He might have been preparing a detailed memorandum on her, and mentally she began to write it for him.

Hair—warm blonde under perched pillbox hat. Face—triangular. Skin—fresh, faintly dusted with freckles. Eyes—grey, largish. Mouth—call it 'generous' to be kind. Figure—but for some reason she didn't want to find words for his assessment of curves and slimness and carriage. From shoulders to ankles it was a clothes-stripping gaze, and angrily she flushed beneath it, feeling—revealed.

Suddenly the gaze dismissed its interest in her looks, and he said, stating, not asking, 'Miss Kane. So you understood the reference in my advertisement and acted accordingly—one of very few women who did, none of them suitable, according to Scott, Burlap and Burlap, who've weeded through the applicants, male and female, for me.

The males, I'm afraid, had to go their way. I needed a member of your sex for the slightly unorthodox duties I had in mind, but you'll understand that our eager beaver women's libbers forbade me to advertise for a Woman Friday as such.'

Danielle inclined her head. 'I know my Robinson Crusoe, and I took a chance on that.'

'Being interested in the job?'

'I shouldn't be here if I weren't.'

He slanted a quick glance at her. 'You have a dry line in repartee,' he commented. 'Another question—which I do *trust* you won't equally despise— what makes you think you could qualify for it?'

His sarcasm hadn't escaped her. All square so far, she thought. Aloud she parried, 'How can I know, until you tell me what it entails?'

His answer to that was to return to his seat behind his desk. Pen in hand, 'Perhaps we could begin with the conventional statistics? Age. Education. Previous posts—as briefly as possible.'

She told him. 'Twenty-three. Grammar school. A-levels in English and French. No employed post as such. Since I left school I've acted as assistant to my aunt in her agency supplying couriers, visiting cooks, theatre tickets, pet-sitters—the lot of people's needs. Filling gaps myself, as often as not.'

'H'm—adaptable. Have you travelled abroad?'

'To most of the neigbouring countries. Escorting children hither and yon.'

'And why aren't you still doing the same work for your aunt?'

Danielle compressed her lips. 'She died. The agency had to fold.'

'A pity. Weren't you equipped to carry it on?'

'No.' She could have enlarged on that to his discomfiture, she could faintly hope. But this was neither the time nor the place.

He was flicking his pen between his fingers. 'And so, being used to filling gaps, as you put it, you weren't dismayed by my needing only "temporary service" of you?' he questioned.

'Not at all,' she agreed, and waited. She would *not* hint again that she would like to know what he wanted of her. She would make him tell her.

In his own time he did, after turning on her again that personal scrutiny which had offended her earlier. Then he was saying crisply, 'Yes, well—I'm in need of a hostess to my guests on a Mediterranean cruise of a few weeks in my yacht *Pandora*, berthed at Southampton. I should expect of her all the functions of a wife if I had one—keeping them amused on board, escorting them in our ports of call, playing *châtelaine* to them, and in particular acting as chaperon to my teenager goddaughter, whom I shall ultimately deliver to her mother in Monte Carlo. Gina—Gina Lisle—is sixteen and has just left boarding school. Could you handle that?'

'I think so. How many other guests would there be?'

'Three for the cruise. A young protégé of mine, a skilled draughtsman between jobs; he and Gina join the yacht at Southampton, and we pick up a man and a woman, in-laws to each other, at Lisbon. But I shall also be entertaining business friends, giving parties for them in some of our ports of call, and you would be overseeing the staff on the catering and so on. The crew, by the way, is all-male, including the cooks.'

'Cooks—in the plural?' Danielle queried.

'Two—for English and Continental cuisines. And if that dismays you, I assure you I need them. My guest list is often considerably longer than the present four names. Well?'

'And you employ a hostess on every cruise you take?'

The tawny eyes narrowed. 'Suggesting that a wife might come cheaper in the long run?' Cabot Steele wanted to know.

Danielle flushed. 'Not at all. Only wondering why, with only four guests permanently aboard, you should need a hostess for this cruise.'

She watched his expression harden. 'My business, surely, if the circumstances of this cruise call for one?' he insinuated coldly.

'I'm sorry——'

He ignored the perfunctory apology to continue, 'I can't commit myself to an exact time schedule for the length of the trip would that matter to you?'

'Not at all.'

'No dates ahead to be cancelled or postponed? With a boy-friend, for instance?'

No business of his, she might well have retorted, but—'I haven't a boy-friend,' she told him.

'Nor close family who need considering in the immediate future?'

'The aunt I've mentioned was my only close relative.'

'Ah, then there probably need be no problem about a further condition of the job, which is that for its duration, you would undertake the role not as my employee but as my fiancée.'

Danielle hardly trusted her ears. 'As your— *fiancée?*' she echoed. 'What an extraordinary suggestion!'

'But necessary, I'm afraid.'

'Why?'

Cabot Steele shrugged. 'I have my reasons, one of them, believe it or not, being a care for your reputation. I need someone like you on the cruise, but pursued by the Press as my movements are, I can hardly board *Pandora* with a nubile young twenty-three-year-old without Questions Being Asked and Conclusions Being Drawn in every gossip column on the news stands. Your name would quickly be mud.'

'Why should it be? If you had to explain me at all, you need only tell the truth—that I'd be your goddaughter's companion for the trip,' Danielle protested.

The analytical, measuring glance swept her again. 'And be believed—about someone of your youth and attraction? My dear, you've evidently never been at the receiving end of all that the gutter-hounds can make up, once they feel they're on a scent!'

Danielle snapped, 'I never have, thank goodness. But if you foresaw that I'd be dragged into the public eye along with yourself, why consider anyone like me for the job in the first place?'

Head at an angle, he considered the question, then remarked at a tangent, 'Wasn't it Julius Caesar who wanted men about him that were fat? Perhaps I could claim that, when I must have women about me, I prefer potential pin-ups to hags—no?'

She thought of the lovely in the outer office and saw his point. But she slung her bag over her arm and prepared to rise. 'I'm afraid we're wasting each other's time, Mr Steele,' she said loftily. 'I think——'

'You don't!' The curt interruption took her aback. 'You're intrigued, interested, even flattered——'

'I am *not* flattered!'

'But you're agog for the details of my bizarre suggestion. You'd specially like to know what I'd pay for such a service. So come, let's talk money. Name your fee?'

She didn't know how she had let him dictate to her so. But since she had, she thought of a figure which would have satisfied her on the job as he had first outlined it; thought of it and trebled it.

His eyebrows peaked. 'That would cover your acceptance of all the conditions I've made?'

'Not the last one! My reputation doesn't need protection.'

'And mine is past recovery? However, I've sprung the idea too suddenly. You need to know more, and time to consider. And so——' Standing now, he flicked through the pages of a desk-diary, 'I'm going down to *Pandora* this evening and sleeping aboard her for two nights. I propose you should lunch with me on board tomorrow. You could catch the eleven-thirty express from Waterloo, and I would meet you at the other end. You could make it?'

'Timewise, I could,' she admitted. 'But again you would be wasting effort for both of us. Your final condition is far too—bizarre.'

'Which was my word for it,' he claimed. 'And though it may sound so, I've given you a reason for it.'

Danielle shook her head. 'Hardly a good enough one.'

He went with her to the door and opened it. 'All the same, I believe at least your curiosity to learn more will take you to Southampton tomorrow.'

'It won't.'

A cynical half-smile twisted his mouth as he gave her his hand. 'I shall meet that train, and I think you'll be on it,' he said.

And she was.

In the interval she had looked at the strange coincidence which had made Cabot Steele, her chosen enemy, the one man in London to offer her an attractive job which she knew she could do, standing on the proverbial one leg, with a hand tied behind her back. From her experience in her aunt's employ she could cater and manage staff, escort and companion, interpret and even fill a vacant chair at a dinner-table. To perform all or any of it in a luxury yacht in the Mediterranean was temptingly exciting, so why—*why* had it to come her way for the taking via that monster of bloated success at his victims' expense, Cabot Steele?

He was a legend everywhere where bricks and mortar and purchaseable land were the stock in trade of his wheeling and dealing. He had the name of a King Midas, everything he touched having turned to the gold of a million by the time he was thirty-five, and that, Danielle suspected, no doubt by the same methods on a large scale as had ruined and served to kill Aunt Catherine on a small.

Looking round the Norwood bedsitter which was now her home, and staring blindly at its ceiling during a largely sleepless night, Danielle had envisaged and regretted yet again that humble relic of an earlier architecture, the shabby terrace of Georgian houses of which her aunt's office had been the centre house, and her and Danielle's home.

Neither it nor its fellows had fallen easily to the Steele hammer of destruction. Months, running into years of infighting between solicitors and lawyers, had happened first and before the occupants had, one by one, given up hope and moved elsewhere. Only Aunt Catherine had stood out to the last for her disputed rights of property. And when she gave in and sold to Cabot Steele's consortium at a tenth the price she could have got earlier, she was a sick woman, in debt and having let all her connections slip from her. And when the empty bottle which had held sleeping pills had been found at her bedside, only charity to the dead had decided she had taken the drug by accident.

In Danielle's eyes that made Cabot Steele responsible for her death, but she had despaired of revenge. Only now—now that she had virtually rejected this ideal job by asking a ludicrously high fee for it, had she been given the chance to say no to him.

But he hadn't allowed her to refuse him finally. By some basilisk-like hypnotism he had left her with the doubt as to whether or not she would be on that Southampton train, by imperiously assuming that she would be.

If she were not, she would enjoy the triumph of her 'No.' But that satisfaction would have manipulated her will so far. But not irrevocably. She could still step back and away from him, and their paths would not be likely to cross again. Curtains. The end of an episode. She would lose face if she gave in.

And yet the man had been craftily right in his claim that she was intrigued by his outrageous 'condition'. She *was* curious about what was behind it, and how he proposed to handle its absurdity. He had promised to tell her if she kept the appointment, and merely going to Southampton would commit her to nothing.

She took the eleven-thirty train.

He was waiting on the station platform, neither his expression nor his greeting to her showing any surprise that she had come. He led the way to his car, saying, 'You'll be ready for your luncheon, I expect. We'll go straight to the mooring bay.'

Danielle could not suppress a gasp when he pointed out the yacht from the quay. It dominated every other berthed cruiser in the bay. She calculated it must be nearly a hundred feet from stem to stern, three decks tall and a-gleam overall with brass and chromium and shining pale grey paintwork. For all its bulk it had a fleet, streamlined look, as if it were already straining to be out to sea.

'Meet *Pandora*,' Cabot Steele introduced her. 'My "floating palace" as the Press cliché has it, though when I'm aboard it's as much my office as my West End premises. That funnel'—he pointed to one of two—'is false. It houses our radio and telex gear, enabling me to do business through any shore-based exchange I need to call. After lunch you must inspect the amenities on offer, to assure yourself that "every home comfort" is laid on.'

For all the world as if I had to be shown the ropes of a job I'd already accepted, thought Danielle as, on deck, he handed her over to a young Malay boy who made up for his lack of English with smiles and gestures, and who squatted on his heels outside the door to wait for her after showing her to a powder-room furnished in pink and silver, and the towels monogrammed C.S.

Luncheon was served on the spacious sundeck in the stern, under an awning. The food was cold— an iced soup, salmon in aspic, with lemon chiffon for pudding. The wine was a dry white St Médoc, and in any other circumstances Danielle could have revelled in the luxury of it all. But by the time the steward had cleared the table and left them to their coffee she was restless under the false pretences of her being there, treated like a guest, and when her host suggested they make a move to explore the yacht, she said firmly, 'If you don't mind, no. She's obviously a fantastic ship, But her geography would only be of concern to me if I were taking the job, and I think I made it clear I couldn't accept the conditions you made?'

'Though if you weren't interested in the details of my proposal, would you be here today?' he countered.

'I—thought I ought to let you enlarge a bit on such a freakish suggestion,' she floundered, only too aware that he had pinpointed her motive as the curiosity it was.

'Which, if you remember, was all I asked,' he returned levelly. 'And so—I've given you one reason for making it. Namely, that as my fiancée, your role as my hostess for the cruise can't be made the subject of sniggering gossip by the public. A lesser one is that, on the voyage itself, as my professional hostess, you could appear as neither crew nor guest, and I'd be reluctant to put you in that questionable position.'

'In other words, "neither fish nor flesh nor good red herring?"' Danielle suggested drily.

He nodded. 'In a nutshell. Again, a third reason—you'll find godchild Gina is neither of an age nor temperament to take the infliction on her of a professional watchdog. She is "agin" authority in any shape, and only her interest in your connection with me is likely to make her accept you or your right to supervise her comings and goings in foreign ports and in a boat with an all-male crew.' He paused and held Danielle's gaze for a long moment. 'Reasons enough? *Good* enough reasons?' he queried.

'They sound plausible,' she allowed.

At that he exploded. 'Plausible be damned! They're true. For heaven's sake, can't you recognise a decent concern that offers you status and authority, and shelter from the wolves always baying at *my* heels? I tell you, it's an essential role for you in the circumstances.'

'And do you have to persuade a fresh hostess to it on every cruise you make?' Danielle asked— unanswerably, she supposed.

'Of course not,' he snapped. 'Escorting Gina is a one-off operation, and even if it weren't, my guest list is usually long enough to include some matron figure who could keep an eye on her.'

'Then couldn't you have———?'

'Laid on a matron to order? No, I could not. This trip isn't a leisure cruise for me. It's a busman's holiday, entailing business on the way, and as I outlined to you, I need more taken from my shoulders than the policing of this teenager. You agreed you could undertake the job as a whole, so may I hope now we can work out the background details?'

'Such as?'

'For instance, how and where we met, got engaged.' He drummed fingers on the table in thought. 'Perhaps in America, which would account for a certain obscurity as to dates and places. Have you been to the States?'

'To Washington for a few days, escorting a diplomat's child home from school in England.'

'That will do. I was in Washington on my last trip over. You are an English girl I met over there, and by coincidence we flew back on the same plane. My courtship of you was swift and too recent even for the newshounds. You *have* to go along with me on this cruise, or be parted from me for as many weeks as I must be away—and that, when we're barely acquainted.' He paused to add, 'For on that, I daresay, you'll have the right to insist—that our passions are still in the dewy stage—so far unconsummated?'

Danielle felt hot colour rise to her cheeks. As calmly as she could she said, 'You're going ahead of me a great deal too fast and too far, Mr Steele. You're assuming I've agreed to be a party to all this, and I haven't, by anything I've said or done. You may be as concerned for me as you say, and I admit I'd like the job very much. But I'd rather cope with whatever it entails under my own steam, without any strings pulled for me by you—do you see?'

It was the first and only time she had appealed to his understanding. But she hadn't reached it. He said on a harsher note than he had used yet,

'If you aren't prepared to accept my terms for the job, then forget it. Make up your mind.' Standing, he went over to the rail and with his back to her, looked out over the water, and in the few minutes which elapsed before he turned again, Danielle, in a breath-catching flash, had realised that this was a chance she mustn't throw away. Until yesterday her enemy standing at the rail had had only a public shape and voice, and if she said no to him now he would never have any more than that. Whereas, in daily touch with him, in his employ on whatever questionable terms, she might learn the more about him which she needed, in order to know what made his ruthless ego tick. He rode roughshod over people's lives, pushed hard bargains for land, razed buildings to the ground for profit, and only in the shipboard dependence and intimacy of weeks which he was offering her could she hope to find out what the man really was—all monster or halfway human. Find out, and use the knowledge, perhaps . . .

When he turned and came back to the table, she said, 'I've made up my mind. I'll take the job.'

'Good.' The crisp monosyllable showed no surprise at her decision. 'You can come aboard a week today?'

'Yes.'

'You'll need an advance on your salary. I'll put in a chit to my accountants about that. What about your wardrobe?'

'My——?'

'The clothes you'll be needing as my fiancée.' He produced a cheque-book, dated and signed a blank and passed it to her. 'You can get all you want at Harridges? If not, let me have any other bills and I'll deal with them.'

Danielle shook her head at the cheque. 'I can't take that.'

'Nonsense. It's an overhead of the job. If you won't——' his eyes, travelling over her, were quizzical, '——I shall enlist the help of a salesgirl of about your figure and buy for you myself, which might not please you at all.' Reaching for her bag, he thrust the cheque into it. 'And so, may I now show you over *Pandora* and let you meet the crew?'

'Just a minute.' She hadn't risen from her chair and had to look up at him.

'Yes?' he invited.

'This "engagement" which we're pretending, how do you suggest it's to be broken off when the time comes?'

'Broken off for public consumption, you mean? Oh, we can give it out that it's by mutual consent. Or you can throw me over, if you'd rather?' he offered.

'At the end of the cruise?'

'Didn't my original advertisement mention that the job was merely temporary?' he returned, his tone cold, almost glacial, and for the first time Danielle experienced a twinge of fear of what she was taking on.

On her next visit to the yacht she was collected in a hired car and driven down to Southampton. Cabot Steele was prevented by business from driving her himself; he would arrive shortly before their evening sailing time, bringing his guest, Simon Milward, with him. Gina Lisle should already be on board, he had told Danielle in one of the several phone calls he had made to her during the week.

During that same week Danielle had admitted to herself that another Danielle Kane had taken over—a new, hard self she hardly recognised but who had pledged her word to Cabot Steele, allowed him to link her name to his, taken his money. That Danielle could afford no more conscience or scruples than need an actor playing the part of a villain for the length of a play's run. So many weeks hence she would be free. But meanwhile she had to keep to the letter of the terms of her hire. *That* Danielle had already managed not to cringe when she had been introduced to the captain of *Pandora* as Cabot Steele's fiancée, nor when an affectionate arm across her shoulders had guided her from one to another of the yacht's luxuries which she would share. The man hadn't kissed her yet, but she supposed that would come . . .

On board she was shown to her cabin, separated from the master bedroom by twin bathrooms, on the top deck. There were flowers in her room, sent by 'him Sahib', according to the steward, who then volunteered, 'Tell Missee Lisle you come aboard, Mem?'

'Please,' said Danielle.

'Will do.'

She had begun to unpack and was hanging up her things in the mirrored wardrobe when, after a perfunctory knock, the door opened and a long-legged girl, barefoot and in a bikini, stood on the threshold. 'I was sunbathing. You wanted me?' she enquired.

'The boy offered to find you,' Danielle put out her hand. 'You're Gina, of course. I'm Danielle.'

The girl flicked a lock of gamin-cut brown hair from her eyes. 'Yes, Cabot's girl. He's only just sprung it that he got engaged in America, and that you'd be coming along this trip. Huh! Cabot engaged—that's a laugh!'

As a speech of welcome it was hardly heart-warming, but Danielle thought it best not question it. She said, 'Well, we did do it all rather in a hurry, and it seemed a good idea to get a bit used to each other on this cruise. And you can imagine my feelings at getting the chance!'

'The chance of swanning it to the Med or of Cabot?'

'Well, of both, I suppose. I'm a very lucky girl.'

'Starry-eyed about him?' Gina asked. 'How odd.'

'Odd?' Danielle queried.

'Well, I mean—*Cabot*.' Gina broke off with a shake of the head. 'Oh, nothing. Forget it—Do you know anything about this jerk he is bringing along for the ride?'

'No. Do you?'

'Only that he's probably one of the youths Cabot collects from time to time. Takes them on as office boys, finds they've got potentials as architects or finance wizards and sends them to university at his expense. This one will wear horn-rimmed specs and he'll stoop——' At another switch of interest Gina pointed to some dresses lying across Danielle's bed. 'They're natty. I like that one. What other clothes have you brought? Let me see.'

The new Danielle had been able to argue that Cabot Steele was responsible for her lost livelihood as well as for her aunt's death, and she had spent his blank cheque without much compunction. She knew she had taste and she had bought the best of everything she needed. Again it had been like choosing the stage costumes for the character she was going to have to play.

Gina rummaged and inspected and for the most part approved the slacks and dresses she held against herself to judge their effect in the mirror. Of a one-piece swimsuit of which the corsage was merely a criss-cross of revealing strappings, she said, 'You'll have to lie on a beach in that; you can't waste it under water.' And of a chiffon evening dress shading from palest azure to night-dark blue at the swirling hem, 'That'll be an eyeful for Louise Diego. Hope I'm there to see her grinding her teeth!'

Danielle recognised the name. 'You mean Cabot's guest who's joining us at Lisbon?' she asked, realising it was the first time she had used Cabot's Christian name aloud.

'Uh-huh. And Felipe Diego—her brother-in-law,

not her husband. He stays at home to mind the shop.'

'The—shop?'

'Oh, you know—the business. They're big timber exporters and Cabot has a lot of dealings with them. I haven't met Felipe, or his brother Carlos. Only Louise. They're Portuguese, of course. Louise is English.'

'And you think she might envy me that dress?'

Gina nodded. 'Sure thing—with you inside it.'

'Why me?'

'Ask yourself,' said Gina cryptically, and changed the subject again. 'Cabot says he wants you and me to be buddies. But you're so much older that you'll probably try to boss me around, and I warn you, I'm not taking that.'

Danielle smiled. 'I don't know that I'm the bossy type. But if I try it on, you must let me know.'

'You can bet on that,' Gina assured her emphatically. 'Though with Senhora Diego jealous of me, and you with your hackles up, what sort of a trip am I going to have?' Danielle teased.

'And Cabot needing to keep all his plates spinning at once, like the chap at the circus,' Gina supplemented. 'But you did ask for it, didn't you? You've only yourself to blame.'

'To blame for what?' Danielle felt her blood chill.

'For falling so fast for Cabot, so fast that you couldn't wait to get engaged, regardless.'

'Regardless?'

'Well, of all the enemies you could be making, all the women who've missed out on getting Cabot for themselves—Louise Diego, for one.'

'But you said she was married!'

Gina shrugged her narrow shoulders. 'Does it make all that difference, these days?'

Shocked, her tone sharper than she intended, Danielle snapped, 'It should, and anyone of your age ought to want to believe it, I'd have thought.'

'Now you've *gone* all moral and bossy,' Gina grumbled with a pout.

'I'm sorry,' said Danielle. 'But really you've no right to prejudice me against Senhora Diego before we've even met.'

'Except that it won't be long before she does it herself,' Gina retorted. 'I must say I don't envy Cabot. He probably had this trip laid on before he met you, and now, because of the business he does with the Diegos, he can't get out of it. In fact'—head on one side, eyes narrowed, she appeared to ponder—'could be, though he told me, and probably you too, that he wanted you along to keep me in order, his real idea was to use you—use his engagement to you, I mean, as—cover.'

CHAPTER TWO

AND that, thought Danielle in a dazzling flash of insight which she did not share with the girl, was exactly what Cabot Steele did want of her.

Not as a guide to his party when he was too occupied to take them about; not as a hostess; not as chaperon to Gina. Not for any purpose but to guard him from the scandal of sharing the intimacy of his yacht with a woman who wanted him, a woman who, married to a Latin, must be sheltered from scandal herself; probably a woman by whose attraction he was enough tempted to be aware that only through his supposed engagement could they both escape the suspicion of conducting an affair which, publicly, they couldn't afford.

But though that was what Gina, cynical beyond her years, must have meant by 'cover' Danielle would not take her up on it. She must not gossip about Cabot's suspect intentions; she must not let Gina suppose she would believe anything but good of the man to whom she was engaged. Outwardly at least, she had to be on Cabot's side.

She said lightly, 'We *are* letting our imaginations run riot, aren't we? In a matter of minutes we've got Senhora Diego jealous, and Cabot weaving dark plots. How he'd laugh if he knew the complications we've thought up to enliven the trip!'

Gina turned on her too quickly. 'You aren't

going to tell him what I've said?'

'Do you imagine I should?' Danielle countered. 'That *would* be a way of setting us all off on the wrong foot!'

'Yes—well,' said Gina, mollified, 'I was only trying to put you in the picture. But naturally you won't hear a word against Cabot, and why should you? You must still be floating on Cloud Nine.'

Cloud Nine indeed! When Gina had wandered off, Danielle saw she was faced by three possible courses. She could repack and walk off the yacht before Cabot joined it. But before they had parted at Southampton she had signed an agreement which bound them both to abide by the terms of their contract until such time as he had no further use for her services. If she broke that, there could be untold legal consequences, and besides, she had a rooted respect for her given word.

She could take him up on his wilful deception of her—accuse him to his face. But that would be acting only on her intuition and Gina's hearsay, neither of which might stand close scrutiny at this stage.

Or she could keep her promise of silence to Gina; accuse Cabot of nothing until she had more evidence of his intrigue; allow him to suppose she had had no reason for second thoughts on their pact since they had last met.

Deciding on that third course, she was aware of a tinge of suspicion that she had chosen it out of a strange reluctance to abandon her original purpose of finding some vulnerable chink in her enemy's armour at which she might strike in some as yet unforeseen way. Fate had thrown Cabot Steele into her path, and there was a pull, a compulsion about keeping him there . . .

She was on the sundeck, getting the last of the evening sun, when he came aboard with the young man Simon Milward, who neither stooped nor wore horn-rims, but was a slim fair-bearded youth with a retiring air. Cabot, in short-sleeved, open-necked shirt and light slacks, had sloughed his city executive appearance along with his formal clothes. As he came towards her, Danielle could not deny that, easily clad as now, he had a dark attraction. Glimpsed across a party room or on a dance floor, he was a man she would have liked to know—if she hadn't already known what he was in his public role of tycoon. Now she supposed she might be in the way of learning how much he was the hard-headed businessman, how much the practised seducer, and how very little he had been concerned for *her* reputation when he had beguiled her into the job.

With a hand on her shoulder to prevent her rising from her sunlounger, he bent to kiss her lightly in front of the boy and Gina, who strolled down the deck to join them.

He introduced Simon—'In his spare time he'll be doubling as my secretary'—kissed Gina and ruffled her cap of damp hair, and told Danielle, 'We must drink to our first night on board. But I must see Boss Fortescue first to agree on sailing time, and then I'd like to shower and change. Have they housed you next to me, as I told them to? Good. Then give me, say half an hour, and come and see me in my cabin when I'm halfway decent.'

So this was the mask of intimacy he expected

her to accept! Danielle smiled her agreement to join him, but her pulse, which had quickened at his kiss, was thudding a warning now. How far did he intend this charade of an engagement to take them?

When she went up on deck his cabin door was open and, changed into a corded silk jacket and bow tie, he was sitting on his bed, thumbing through some papers. He put them aside and took her by the hand. 'Fortescue is just about to take her out,' he said. 'Come along to the bridge and watch the operation.'

There was an exciting judder underfoot, orders shouted. Orders being confirmed, lights flashing into the twilight, the hoot of a siren, and then slow movement under controlled power, and *Pandora* was slipping down the Solent, heading for the open sea.

Cabot sighed with satisfaction as he turned from the rail and took Danielle's arm on their way down to the lounge for drinks. 'I find it as stimulating for the umpteenth time as for the first,' he said. 'What about you?'

'For me it *is* the first time,' she admitted.

'Putting out to sea? Surely not?'

'In a yacht like this,' she explained. 'And one usually travels by air nowadays.'

'Not I, if I can help it,' he denied. 'Speed is the only consideration which will get me on to an aircraft in order to cross the sea. Can anyone say they really enjoy the boredom of flying?'

'I can,' she claimed. 'But on journeys of only a few hours, except the once I went to America and back.'

'Ah, that trip—we mustn't forget that we travelled together on that return journey,' he warned. He touched the fingers of her left hand. 'I see you haven't provided yourself with a ring from a chainstore. Didn't Gina notice you weren't wearing one?'

'If she did, she didn't mention it.'

'I'm surprised she didn't want to Ooh and Aah over your symbol of bondage to me. Anyway, the omission will be rectified. I had to guess at your taste in stones; also at your size. But that can be put right at Lisbon if necessary.'

She drew away from him as far as his hold would permit. 'Isn't that taking a lie rather far?' she queried.

'Necessary thinking for you, I'm afraid. The absence of a ring could take some embarrassing explanation,' he retorted. 'Meanwhile, you've rehearsed "Cabot," I hope?'

'I've used it to Gina,' she replied shortly.

'As I've used "Danielle" to the newshounds.'

She halted. 'You've talked to reporters *already*?'

He urged her forward. 'They've talked to me, baying on the trail of rumour and the announcement in yesterday's *Times*. But don't worry. I sent them away satisfied that propriety was being served and this was an introduction to *Pandora* for you, not a pre-nuptial orgy.'

Avoiding admitting what it's to be for you and Senhora Diego, if Gina is right, was Danielle's suspicious thought as he swung open the door of the dining saloon for her and they went in.

Captain Fortescue and his first officer dined with them and Gina and Simon Milward. The talk between the men was mostly of *Pandora*'s affairs; once during dinner Cabot was called from the table by the radio officer; Gina and the boy made halting acquaintance of each other, reminding Danielle of the circling of young dogs, none too sure whether to snap or to frolic.

The officers left to take coffee in their own mess and Cabot dismissed the two young people with the suggestion that Gina should show Simon over the yacht.

Gina wanted to linger. 'He can see it tomorrow just as well,' she objected.

'And I'd like to be alone with Danielle, if you don't mind.'

'Oh well——' she hitched a shoulder in acceptance. 'But come and find me when you've——finished. I've had a letter from Mother I want you to see.'

Cabot and Danielle moved to the lounge to the comfort of deep armchairs rioting with bright scatter cushions and soundproofing from the beat of the engines. Cabot drew up a chair at right angles and close to Danielle's. 'I wonder what we were being allowed to "finish,"' he said with a dry chuckle. 'Some torrid excess better confined to a bedroom, or what?' He watched as Danielle was aware she had flushed. 'You blush charmingly,' he commented. 'One had been told it was a lost art.'

He stretched his legs and clasped his hands behind his head. 'You've talked to Gina? How did you get on?'

'I was warned against being bossy.'

'I expected you would be. And if I'd offloaded on her a real battleaxe of a duenna, the poor woman mightn't even have been warned. She'd have been told exactly where she got off.'

'What makes Gina so prickly?'

'M—mm—she's that sort of age, I suppose. And she's got problems,' Cabot said, without enlarging on what they were.

Danielle waited, then asked, 'Oughtn't I to know what they are?'

'I think I'll let her confide them to you, if she wants to.'

'I see. And supposing——' Danielle began on a question she didn't know how to put—'supposing you hadn't found anyone to chaperon her as suitable as you say you found me, what then?'

'You mean, if a selection of middle-aged dragons had answered my advertisement? I'd have had to wait for you.'

'For someone like me, you mean?'

For an inscrutable moment the tiger eyes held hers. 'I'd have waited for you,' he said.

It was an absurd answer to her reasonable question. Without knowing of her existence, how could he have waited for her in person? But of course he must have meant he had needed some girl of the right age and appearance to be passed off as his fiancée for his own self-interested ends. His emphatic insistence that he had waited for her had merely been a subtle piece of flattery which would have pleased her, had he been any other than the man he was.

He was saying next, 'It's as well we took the precautions we did. They're investigating and describing you with enthusiasm.'

'By "they", you mean the reporters? How do you know?'

'By radio. I was called to take some messages at dinner, if you remember? They're going to town with happy propriety about "Cabot Steele's lovely fiancée" instead of all the snide innuendoes they'd have indulged about his latest "good friend".' At Danielle's quick frown of distaste, he added, 'Which reminds me, I don't know enough of your background myself for comfort—where you were born, your family and so on?'

She gave him a few bare details—her father a Naval doctor who had gone down with his ship, her mother a Naval nurse who had caught a tropical bug from a patient. That brought her to her life with her aunt and the danger of enlarging more upon that than she cared to as yet. She wanted to hug to herself the promise of a time when she would tell him just why she had accepted his job— for vengeance' sake, to live alongside and analyse his ruthlessness, and to milk him of as much money as would compensate in small part for her loss of livelihood. On that day she would make it clear she hadn't been deceived at all by his claim to be concerned for her good name. So she told him no more than she had originally of the cause of the break-up of her home and her work.

'And recreations?' he invited.

'Swimming, travel, if it hadn't been part of my job, the theatre when I can afford it, riding ditto.'

'Friends—of both sexes? No boy-friend at the moment, I think you said? But past rivals to my alleged conquest of you—there have been some?'

She looked him straight in the eye. 'I'm twenty-three,' she said with oblique meaning, and he laughed.

'The snub direct? Or the provocative hint?' And at another irritable frown from her, 'All right, you don't have to admit which. I'll look forward to finding out for myself,' he said.

He switched to asking if her escort work had ever taken her to Lisbon. When she said no, he rose. 'Let's see what the library has to offer. I daresay you'd like to know something about it before we get there. We shall be two or three days in port, and there'll be some entertaining for us laid on.'

The library's walls were lined with books and there was a built-in TV screen. Cabot chose for her a guide to Portugal and a chatty travel book of a small yacht under sail on much of *Pandora*'s route from England to the Riviera. He stood close at her shoulder as she examined both books, his nearness an intimacy she couldn't avoid when he turned pages for her or pointed to sketch-maps. Briefly she was not on her guard against him. They were just two people talking books, agreeing and differing with an ease which disarmed her hostility while it lasted.

'I'd like to borrow both these,' she said, closing them and turning—in that narrow space, almost into his arms.

'Do,' he said, and took them from her. 'I'll drop them in at your cabin on my way to find Gina. You won't be going to bed yet?'

'But I think I shall.'

'Then I'll come along with you.'

At her door he handed back the books and left her with a cool, 'Sleep well, your first night aboard,' which showed, she thought thankfully, remembering his kiss in front of Gina and Simon, that he meant to keep any pretence of intimacy for public display only. She would be prepared to settle for that. If he didn't overdo it, she would learn not to cringe . . .

When she had undressed she wasn't really ready for sleep, so she put on the matching negligé of her ruffled cotton nightgown and sat down to read the travel book. It was full of incident and held her attention until, half an hour or so later, there were voices outside her door. With a thumb keeping her place, she listened, heard Gina laugh and Cabot speak. Then there was a knock and Gina looked round the door to claim, 'There! What did I tell you? She's been waiting up to say goodnight properly. So come on and do your engaged stuff, Cabot Steele. *I'm* going to bed!'

She ducked under Cabot's arm higher up the door and disappeared as Danielle stood, drawing the light robe round her and as Cabot came in, leaving the door to half-close behind him.

'Gina considers I'm neglecting the courtesy of tucking you into bed and kissing you goodnight,' he said. 'So may I stay long enough to appear to be doing just that?'

Danielle stiffened. 'You shouldn't have invited her to express her opinion.'

'As if today's teenagers wait for invitation to anything, their business or not,' he scoffed. 'And in the circumstances I'd have looked pretty churlish if I'd refused.'

'Need you have put yourself in the way of having to refuse? You could have said you knew that by this time I'd be in bed and asleep.'

'Which, fortunately, you're not.'

'*Fortunately?*'

'As it happens. Because it affords me the chance to give you your rights.' He came across to her, taking a jewel-box from his pocket. 'Not later than tomorrow's breakfast-time Gina will expect you to be wearing this. And so——'

Danielle's eyes were drawn down to the magnificent square-cut solitaire diamond in its velvet bed. 'I can't even pretend to own that,' she protested. 'It's too—extravagant by far.'

'Don't worry, it will be adequately insured.'

She bit her lip. 'I didn't mean extravagant in money, but as I've said before, to expect me to flaunt a ring like that is taking the whole charade of our engagement too far.'

'And as I've told *you* before, you could suffer more embarrassment without it than with it.' He reached for her hand, slid the ring into place and turned it to test its fit, which happened to be perfect. 'Why do you make such heavy weather of all this?' he asked. 'It's only a matter of convenience for us both, so why not accept it and enjoy it?'

'*Is* it possible to enjoy deceiving people?' she retorted sharply.

'Why not, if it serves a purpose and harms no one? Do you suppose sleight-of-hand magicians don't enjoy their work, and there's no reason why we shouldn't enjoy ours while the necessity is there. For instance, there'll be the duty endearment and the duty kiss, but we needn't make a distasteful burden of them . . . need we?'

In his pause his arm had drawn her effortlessly

to him and she guessed where his question was leading. Warmly moist, exploratory, his lips found hers, their heat and their pressure demanding, rather than inviting, her response.

It was no duty kiss, nor yet the tentative first kiss of lovers. It was experienced, sensual, passionate as it deepened, holding her in thrall to a compulsion to savour its pleasure to the full. By no means her first kiss of many from the men she had known, but the only one which had so stirred her senses to an almost unbearable height of excitement. And that, from a man she had every cause to hate How could her body betray her so?

The arm about her waist hadn't moved, but when at last he released her lips, the fingers of his other hand traced the line of her jaw and throat and lingered at the cleavage above the frills of her low-cut nightgown. 'Not bad for a first encounter of a strictly carnal kind. And they do say practice makes perfect,' he murmured.

At that her excitement chilled. Anger and sanity took over.

'There won't be any more practice of that sort,' she said.

Cabot let her go and stood back. 'Oh, I don't know. Our image may need it. It depends on how quick a study you are,' he drawled. And with satyric cruelty as he went out, 'After all, what am I paying you for?'

Danielle dropped upon her bed, humiliated and ashamed. At their first meeting the man's appraisal had seemed to strip her, and now the physical desire he had roused in her had done much the same. She had laid herself open to his easy conquest of her senses, and she was convinced his experience had known just how vulnerable, in that mood, she was. He hadn't pretended to be making love to her; his mocking use of 'carnal' told that. He had merely been exercising a sexual power to which she shouldn't have fallen victim. That she had, and had let him know it, was a self-rancour she couldn't forget.

And what did his emphasis on their masquerade prove? Surely that its success had more importance for him than that Gina's hostility for a professional chaperon for the voyage should be disarmed? Nor could it matter *so* much that her own standing should be above suspicion. No, the more she pondered it, the more she was inclined to share Gina's suspicion—that it was cover for quite another affair. Pending? Or already in being? How could she tell?

She slept only fitfully and had already been about when her morning tea was brought. From her porthole to starboard she had glimpsed an open sea as calm and blue as the sky. Cabot had said overnight that, cruising at about ten knots, *Pandora*'s timing to Lisbon should be something over three days, and Danielle supposed that he would brief her this morning on her expected duties until then. She wasn't looking forward to the interview at all, but when he rose from the breakfast table saying easily to her, 'You don't have to run any part of the show if you'd rather laze. But if you want to take a hand, suppose we get together on the sundeck in, say, half an hour, and we'll see where you could help?' she realised that, for Gina's hearing, her co-operation as his fiancée was being asked, not her obedience ordered, and that, in case Gina chose to occupy the sundeck too, mention of last night's scene was taboo.

In fact Gina was not present, but she could have been, for Cabot had summoned both chefs for consultation, suggesting that Danielle might like to see them each morning to discuss menus. As she would need to be familiar with the stores, he handed over the keys to her. He himself saw to the wines and superintended the Customs bonding of them in port. Was there anything else he could do for Danielle or Gina? No? Well, the swimming pool would be filled by the afternoon, and he and Simon Milward would join them there for an hour. Meanwhile he had to brief Simon on his work and would be occupied until luncheon. It was all as clinical and impersonal as a board meeting, causing Danielle to wonder whimsically why Simon hadn't been present to record the minutes. Only Cabot's hand trailed across her shoulders as he left the deck had given any sign of their supposed intimacy. Last night might never have happened.

She went with the chefs to marvel at the equipment of the galley, where the ovens were all wall-set under hods, the cooking utensils all of copper and the stowage of everything a miracle of ingenuity. When she remarked on this to the English chef he said dryly, 'We've had to cross Biscay in winter as well as in summer, and having his Royal Worcester and his cut glass hurled off shelves is something the Chief wouldn't find funny, madam.'

The stores' cupboards were an Aladdin's cave of enough supplies for at least two months, Danielle calculated, and the freeze units were packed to capacity.

All this, she mused—all this and a swimming pool and live and video-recorded TV and state suites and a library and radio by satellite and a speedboat and a tender—all of it purchased and enjoyed at the price of victims like Aunt Elizabeth. Cabot Steele's parade of wealth had a lot to answer for indeed!

At lunch he repeated his intention to be at the pool in the afternoon, but perversely Danielle decided she wouldn't be there. She told Gina she was going to read and perhaps take a nap in her cabin, and in this she wasn't disturbed. In the late afternoon she got up and went fully dressed to the pool, to find only Simon Milward there, doing a lazy crawl stroke from one side to the other.

At sight of her he sprang out and reached for his towel. 'Mr Steele had to go back to work. Shall I tell him you're here now?' he asked.

'No, don't bother. I'm not swimming now,' she said, and then, 'We've hardly had a word with each other, have we? Won't you stay and tell me a bit about yourself?'

'Oh—well.' Danielle wouldn't have said a youth of his age could blush, but he did. He continued to towel himself, then sat down cross-legged on the pool surround. 'What about me?' he asked.

'Well, you're a draughtsman between jobs, Cabot says——'

'Out of work. There's a difference.'

'Yes, I know. But you're filling in with some work for my fiancé?'

'He's putting up with me.' Simon paused. 'What else have you heard about me?'

'Nothing, I think.'

'Not that I was a drop-out from an architect's office and that I only kicked drugs three months ago?'

Danielle denied, 'Cabot wouldn't have passed on anything like that. He wouldn't think it any of my business, and when I asked you about yourself I wasn't prying. I think I wanted to hear about your family and how you came to know Cabot —things of that sort.'

'My family emigrated, but I wouldn't go. And I belonged to one of Mr Steele's youth clubs for a time—you know, he sponsors clubs all over the place?'

It was something of Cabot's leisure activities which Danielle should have known of. 'Yes, of course,' she improvised hastily. 'Which one?'

'In Balham. Has he taken you to it?'

'Not yet. We've been engaged such a little while.'

'Yes, well—I dropped out of the club too when I went on the drug scene, and when Mr Steele missed me—he takes karate classes—he came after me and almost literally hauled me out of the gutter by my ear. Since then he's kept an eye on me, sent me to night school to take my Guilds. If I get them he'll take me on in the Cabot Steele drawing offices. Always supposing I keep off the drugs, of course.'

'And you mean to?'

He stood up in a lithe easy movement. 'There's no way I'll go back to them. I wouldn't have Mr Steele despise me that much,' he said. And then,

'You don't have to tell Gina Lisle all this, do you?'

'Of course not,' Danielle agreed. 'Tell her just as much as you want her to know. Do you think you are going to get on with her on the trip?'

Simon pulled a face. 'Couldn't say. So far I'm a bit of a non-person; she'd as soon have my room as my company.'

'And you?'

'She's all right, I suppose,' he allowed. 'Though mind you, I've seen better pin-ups by far!'

When he had gone Danielle looked at this new facet of Cabot Steele. An athlete, a benefactor. Strangely, none of his publicity had featured this. Which meant he must have forbidden its mention, or the newshounds would have made a meal of this contradiction to his image as a single-minded pursuer of success at any price. Without its ever reaching the headlines, a lot of time and money must have gone to the sponsorship of, according to Simon, more than one youth club, and Danielle found she was wondering what difference, if any, Simon's story had made to her own view of her enemy. None, she wanted to believe, but her curiosity was heightened.

She was not to see Cabot alone that evening, except for a few minutes before dinner, when he said curtly, 'I'd hoped to spend the afternoon with you. Were you deliberately avoiding me?'

Resenting his tone, she shrugged. 'Deliberately? I suppose I was,' she agreed.

'And what does that mean?'

'Well, that I didn't happen to stay in my cabin to rest by accident. It was a decision,' she said.

'Not a very wise one on our first day at sea,' he

snapped back as Gina and then Simon joined them.

After dinner the yacht's library provided a recorded film they all wanted to see. It was not over until eleven o'clock, when they parted for the night. In her cabin Danielle debated locking her door, but decided that was a defeatist tactic. She must not rely on bolts and bars to show Cabot he couldn't have his way with her as and when he pleased. If he came she would have to play the situation by ear; in fact, she was half looking forward to another clash of their wills—as long as she emerged the winner.

She was awake until after midnight in expectancy. But he did not come.

Cabot's claim that for him the cruise was only a busman's holiday was borne out during the two days before the yacht made Lisbon. He saw Captain Fortescue each morning after breakfast, then he and Simon worked until noon at correspondence and taking and sending radio calls. They would appear briefly for pre-lunch drinks, join Danielle and Gina at the pool or on the sundeck in the afternoon—sessions from which Danielle did not defect again—and worked again until dinner. On neither night did Cabot go to Danielle's cabin, but bade her an affectionate goodnight when she chose to go to bed. It was a régime which made Gina grumble on her behalf, 'Super kind of engagement trip he's giving you! If he hadn't given you a diamond the size of a roc's egg, no one could blame you for wondering if his heart is really in it. Aren't you beginning to say, Roll on, Lisbon, where there should be some parties and *men*? I am, even with La Diego and her stooge in prospect for the rest of the way, and surely Cabot will ease up a bit then?'

Danielle defended Cabot. 'He warned me that it had to be a working affair for him, and that's partly why I came along, to take some of the yacht's domestic things off his shoulders.'

'Making use of you!' Gina scoffed. 'You should have refused and told him, No way.'

Danielle laughed. 'But I wanted to come,' she pointed out.

'And fell over yourself letting him know it, I bet!'

'I daresay,' Danielle said carelessly, and then cancelled the lie with the truth, 'I don't know that Cabot gave me much chance to refuse.'

'Masterful, hm? Well, they say women like to be dominated. But just let any male try to dominate *me*!' Gina claimed.

The shipping lanes became increasingly busy as *Pandora* neared Lisbon, and though she could have docked on the night of the third day out from Southampton, Captain Fortescue stood off from the mouth of the Tagus until dawn of the next day. As she made her way up to the Belem yacht quays there was a view of the whole city, spread white and glistening in the morning sunlight on the slopes of its many hills. South across the river there were glimpses of the long golden sands of Estoril, where in its hinterland the Diego brothers had their *quinta* on the edge of the forests of timber they owned.

Cabot had business at the docks and was not ready to escort his party ashore until noon. A long open chauffeured car awaited them at the dock gates; it was to be at Cabot's disposal throughout the visit. For lunch at the Quinta Laura Danielle had chosen a blue sailor suit faced with white and a stiff straw boater with ribbon streamers. Gina, under protest, was wearing a dress for once.

'Why not slacks and a shirt?' she had grumbled. But Danielle had prevailed with the argument that they couldn't turn up like tramps, adding with guile, 'As you don't seem to care for Senhora Diego, do you want her to think you've nothing but deck gear to wear?'

The *quinta*, facing into the sun and backed by dark pines, was the typical estate manor, long, low and white, the length of its façade shaded by a pillared colonnade. At the main open doorway two men and a woman were waiting as the car drew up.

Cabot was out and handing out Danielle and Gina. The older man came forward, both hands outstretched in greeting; the younger followed. There was a continental embrace for Cabot; then he bent to put his lips to the woman's hand before drawing Danielle to his side.

'Louise, Carlos, Felipe—meet Danielle Kane, my fiancée, please,' he announced, and watched the men look their surprise.

It was Louise Diego who spoke. Offering a limp hand to Danielle, she said, 'Your *fiancée*, Cabot? This is—news.'

CHAPTER THREE

NOT good news, nor bad news, but news which Louise Diego did not welcome, was Danielle's impression, and a snort of mirth from Gina implied that she thought so too.

'Mean to say you hadn't *heard*?' she gloated. 'You should take a look at the ring he's given her. It's out of this world!'

'Really?' Louise managed a thin smile for Danielle and turned to the men. 'No, we hadn't heard, had we, Carlos?—Felipe? We get our social news from the English papers' weekly editions, and you, Cabot, haven't seen fit to tell us, have you? Not a word from England before you sailed, and not a murmur on your radio calls from *Pandora* since! Such a way to treat old friends! Anyone would think you had something to hide about the affair; that it was shotgun, or that you'd be marrying beneath you. Whereas——' a graceful hand drew Danielle into the circle—'Miss Kane is quite beautiful and altogether too good for you—do you know that?'

'I know it,' Cabot agreed. As the men congratulated him, he went on, 'It wasn't shotgun, but it was sudden—"at first sight" and so on, and I kept it under wraps in England until we sailed and escaped the brouhaha. Once the story was out, I couldn't leave her behind to face it alone, so I brought her along to sample the cruising I hope we

46

shall be doing and to give her a taste of home-making on *Pandora* for practice.'

'And for practice in other arts too, no doubt,' Louise hinted, her wan smile suddenly turned brilliant. Then she was noticing Simon and asking for him to be introduced, and reminding Gina of their last meeting in England when Gina had still been at school. And now imagine! Gina was on the way to being grown-up! At which sally Gina retorted, 'I don't have to imagine it. I am grown-up—ask Mother.'

They adjourned for drinks to a patio shaded by a grapevine, and under cover of the general talk in which she wasn't always involved Danielle took stock of their hosts and hostess.

Carlos Diego was her idea of the typical *hidalgo*—poker-erect, goatee-bearded and darkly bronzed. His brother was very different, with pale hair sleeked back from a backward-sloping forehead. His eyes were a cold slate and he had a curiously empty face. She disliked his thick lips and his fat hands, which he used too freely in contact with Louise's and Gina's and her own.

Both men spoke fluent English with ease.

Louise Diego was slim, tall, with a golden-bronze skin and hair as black, with blue lights, as if she too were Portuguese or Spanish. She wore her hair today smoothly centre-parted and twisted into a chignon drawn to one side below her ear. It was a variation of the ballet-dancer's knot, and Danielle guessed Louise had made the style unique to herself.

She wore a close-fitting suit of scarlet silk and the heels of her scarlet sandals were three inches high. She used expressive hands, the slow turn of her head, the droop and lift of her eyelids, all in the cause of a seductive invitation at which she was adept. Even her husband, Danielle noticed, watched her adoringly, seeming oblivious that her art was directed at Cabot and Felipe and Simon Milward.

How false it all was, thought Danielle. Cabot's enthusiasm for their supposed engagement, Louise Diego's flattery which had contradicted her dismayed reception of the news, Danielle's own acceptance of a way of life which would never have been hers if she weren't playing the game of deception too. This was the web into which she had allowed Cabot Steele to lure her, and now she was as guilty as he.

Presently they lunched on cucumber salad garnished with chopped mint, a Portuguese dish, a kind of fish risotto, and a coffee soufflé for pudding. Afterwards the Diego men and Cabot departed to talk business; Louise told Simon, 'I'm sure you don't want to be bored with women's talk, so do go and explore the grounds if you would like to,' and Gina claimed, 'I'll go with him', leaving Danielle and their hostess to a tête-à-tête.

Watching Gina as she strolled away to join Simon Louise remarked, 'What a truly uncouth child she is! Don't they teach them any manners at expensive boarding schools nowadays? At lunch she was pert with Cabot, and she snubs that young man unmercifully. What was Cabot's idea in bringing him along? Is he hoping they'll make a match, do you know?'

'Good heavens, I shouldn't think so,' Danielle exclaimed.

Louise's eyes narrowed. 'But you don't *know*?' she pressed, and Danielle saw her mistake. As Cabot's fiancée she should have known what were his plans for Simon and Gina if he had any. So she quickly amended, 'I mean, I'm sure Cabot doesn't expect that. Simon hasn't a job at present and he's not much more than a boy, and Gina is only sixteen.'

'But already a woman of the world in her own eyes. You heard her claim that to me, and that her mother would confirm it.'

'Yes, though I didn't know what she meant when she said "Ask my mother," Danielle admitted.

The other woman's graceful head moved slowly from side to side in reproof. 'Dear me, you *have* let Cabot keep you in the dark, haven't you? Do you mean he hasn't told you about Mrs Lisle's financial difficulties which she plans to solve by marrying Gina off to some rich Swiss banker she's keeping on ice for the child? Really, since he confided in me the last time we met, I'd have thought he would tell you! But there—I suppose you're still so wrapped up in each other that you talk of nothing but yourselves. Tell me, how long after you met him did Cabot propose?'

With ironic truth Danielle said, 'Very soon.'

'And you both *knew*,' Louise breathed. 'How I recognise that feeling of oneness with a man! I know I experienced it in the little nonsense of an affair I had with Cabot before I married Carlos, which of course is *the real thing*!' She paused. 'You mustn't mind that tiny confession, for it really was a nothing, of no consequence at all. You do understand? Or has Cabot told you already that we were rather close for a little time, while it lasted?'

'If it mattered to either of you more than you say, he would have told me, I'm sure,' said Danielle, sure of no such thing.

'Of course. And he wouldn't have risked making you jealous for no reason,' Louise agreed smoothly. 'I hear we're to dine with you in *Pandora* tomorrow night. I suppose Cabot has brought along a butler or somebody to handle his entertaining?'

'No, he's letting me be in charge of all that. It's what he meant by giving me a taste of homemaking.'

'Oh, my dear, how devious can men get? I shall tell Cabot he has no right to expect you to double up as his housekeeper before he's even married you!'

'But I wanted to show him I could do it. I still do.' To forestall Louise's probing into her domestic experience, Danielle said, 'Do you know, I'd love to see your gardens too. Would it be too much trouble to show me round?'

On their way she had to wish she had Cabot there to satisfy Louise's curiosity about her. Some of the questions she could answer with truth, others she managed to turn aside. But she was made uncomfortably aware of the gaps in her story when, on their return to the house, Louise remarked, 'I shall have to ask Cabot just how he succeeded in keeping you so secretly from us all. Because I've just the *teeniest* suspicion that you're both holding out on us!' It was said lightly with a dazzling smile. But there was meaning behind it which Danielle feared. It was going to tax all Cabot's double-dealing to parry Louise's quizzing. Unless of course—the suspicion flashed—Louise's show of ignorance was a false front in itself, and she knew already from Cabot that his alleged fiancée had been brought on the scene purely as cover for their continuing affair in the comparative privacy of *Pandora*!

If that were so, it made Gina hideously right and the intrigue the deeper. And yet even Gina had only suggested Cabot wanted protection from the scandal of Louise's being aboard without her husband, not that he was promising himself an amorous interlude with Louise. No—Danielle gave herself a mental shake—she must *not* damn Cabot as more than the skilled manipulator he was. Oddly, the thought that she and he might be common allies against Louise Diego's hopes of him did not displease her. It made a kind of bond—their only one . . .

When they returned to the yacht in early evening he apologised to her for the short notice of the next night's dinner party. 'I had to invite some other people by telephone from the Diegos, and tomorrow was the only time they could manage,' he said.

'How many will there be for dinner, then?' Danielle asked.

'To keep the numbers even—eight. Simon can dine in the officers' mess. Put Louise at my right hand; you on my left with Carlos. The Verdes—Ramon Verde can partner Gina, Felipe Diego with Ramon's wife, Pilar. An informal affair, but wear something attractive. Ramon Verde is a dress designer, but he has some spare cash which could find a happy home in Cabot Steele Ltd. and I hope to persuade him so.'

'It will be a business dinner?'

'With its lighter side, as we're evenly matched. We might go into the city or to a nightclub in Estoril afterwards.'

'What would you like the menu to be?'

'That's for you to arrange. But something typically British, I think.'

Danielle agreed. She made a mental survey of the contents of the huge freezer cabinets. 'You could hardly want roast beef or saddle of lamb in this heat, but what about Scotch salmon, with asparagus for the first course and an old English syllabub to follow?'

'Fine.'

'For what time shall I tell the galley?'

'For the meal, not before nine. They eat here as late as the Spaniards do.' Cabot added, 'You ran your first gauntlet with my friends today. How did it go?'

'Distastefully, as far as I was concerned.'

'But convincingly. We offended none of the standards we should have done if I'd had to introduce you as my professional hostess. You wouldn't have liked the consequences of that at all.'

'I'd have felt more honest, at least!'

His expression hardened. 'If all I wanted of you was honesty, you wouldn't be here,' he reminded her. 'I'm paying you more than adequately for a well-intentioned piece of *dis*honesty, and I expect you to keep your side of the pact.'

'Which I have—so far. But that's not to say I'm happy about it.'

He shrugged. 'Your happiness in the part is neither here nor there, I'm afraid. When I'm not satisfied with your playing of it, you can be very sure I shall let you know.'

'I don't doubt it. Didn't you try, my first night on board?' Danielle retorted.

His curt laugh showed he understood her. 'My dear, that was instructive, not corrective—by no means the same thing. I thought I made it clear you were having the first lesson in a course we ought to pursue.' He paused, then urged, 'Come, isn't that your cue for demanding whether I'm issuing a promise or a threat?'

'I shouldn't dream of asking anything so corny,' she denied loftily. 'But for the record you may as well know I don't take at all kindly to threats.'

'No? Though to promises—perhaps?' he insinuated, and left her, seething that she had handed him the opening to snatch the last telling word.

Gina was not at all pleased at Simon's exclusion from the dinner party. Not, she assured Danielle, because she craved his company, but because she would rather have been paired with him than with a stuffy married man she had never met.

'Senhor Verde may not be stuffy, and as it's a Cabot Steele business dinner, Cabot may not want Simon there, as he isn't in the firm yet,' Danielle pointed out.

'Then why should I be at it? I'm not in the firm either. I've a good mind to skip it and get Simon to take me out on the town somewhere,' Gina claimed.

'You'll do nothing of the sort,' Danielle

retorted—too sharply, she realised at Gina's defiant, 'And who says I won't?'

Danielle said, 'Your own good manners should, I'd have thought. You're as much a guest of Cabot's on this trip as—as I am myself, and guests don't throw their host's invitation in his face without good reason.'

'Oh, pooh!' Gina scoffed, but said no more about playing truant.

Danielle chose from her wardrobe of new clothes a svelte dinner dress in lightweight honey-gold velvet with a slashed skirt and plunging neckline. As she laid it on her bed, preparatory to dressing for the evening, Cabot, on his way to his own cabin, stopped by the open door of hers.

'What are you wearing tonight?' he asked.

'That,' she said, and pointed. 'Not in my normal budget, of course. I'm afraid you paid for it. It's a Sericole model.'

'A Sericole?' he echoed sharply. 'You can't wear that!'

She stared. 'Why not?'

'Because, as I told you, I hope to get Ramon Verde's investment in the firm, and I can't have my fiancée parading a model gown from a rival fashion house.' He picked up the dress by its hanger and went to the cupboard to replace it.

Danielle watched him. 'I think that's rather absurd,' she said.

'So you may, but it's business.' He flicked at the skirts of some other dresses. 'Wear one of these instead.'

Not 'Please don't jeopardise my business plans'. Nor 'Do you mind? I'd rather you wore something

else tonight'. But 'You can't.' 'I won't have it'—
orders, not requests; dictation, not appeal. Danielle
bristled at his tone. 'And suppose I choose to wear
the Sericole?' she asked.

They faced each other in cool hostility. Then
Cabot said, 'I think you won't,' and went out,
closing the door behind him.

She was sorely tempted. In fact, she took down
the gold dress again and went about her bathing
and hair and evening make-up, with her mind
closed to any idea of obeying him. But suddenly
the thought struck—*What an out-and-out hypocrite
you are! You lecture Gina on good manners to a
host, so what about your own?* Reluctantly, but
oddly relievedly, she returned the Sericole to the
cupboard and chose an oyster-grey evening blouse
and skirt instead. She explained her relief by telling
herself she was keeping her self-respect, not that
she was truckling to Cabot's orders. But later,
when he was pouring drinks for their guests and
passing her choice to her, he said significantly,
'Thank you,' she felt rewarded.

Socially at least, the dinner was a success. Cabot
was an experienced host, adept at keeping the con-
versational ball on the move and respecting tête-à-
tête talk when he saw it had started up. How successful was the business aspect when the men and
women separated Danielle of course did not know.
She, Louise, Pilar Verde and Gina moved into the
library for their coffee, and after a while she was
able to leave Gina and Louise together when
Senhora Verde asked to be shown over the yacht.
They returned to the library to find the men had
joined them. Cabot suggested 'A film here, or shall

we finish the evening at La Bella Mar?' and yielded to Louise's clamour of 'Oh, La Bella Mar, every time!' without consulting anyone else.

Cabot beckoned Danielle aside. 'La Bella Mar is a gambling night-club and there's a lower age limit of eighteen. Gina can't come,' he said.

'She won't like being told she's too young for anything,' Danielle objected.

'Too bad. Tell her to collect Simon from the mess and they can watch a film or something.'

As Danielle expected, Gina's reaction was characteristically outspoken. 'Am I supposed to be babysitting Simon, or is he babysitting me?' she demanded sulkily.

'You wanted him at the party,' Danielle reminded her.

'Only as an alternative to that pompous stuffed shirt, Senhor Verde. Even *Simon* would be preferable. Anyway, he'd rather stay in the mess, and I shall go to bed with a good book. And you can tell Cabot I hope he has his fill of Louise before the night is out!' was Gina's tart reply.

La Bella Mar, facing its namesake, the beautiful sea, across Estoril's great crescent of golden sands, was brilliantly lit outside, but its public rooms and its casino were left in the discreet shadows of candle lighting. There were tables set around a small dance floor where couples drifted, hardly moving, to dreamy music from a concealed or recorded band. It wouldn't have suited Gina's taste for discothèques, thought Danielle, glad she could tell the girl so.

The casino was more lively, and here Louise came into her own. She seemed to know or be

known by almost everyone as she moved from table
to table, touching people on the shoulder and being
greeted by croupiers and patrons alike.

Her husband said indulgently to Danielle,
'Louise has more time to know and to meet her
friends than I have. But I do know a few of them.
So come and let me introduce them to you and
Cabot—where is he, by the way?'

They looked around. Felipe Diego was nowhere
to be seen. ('At the bar,' judged Carlos.) The
Verdes had taken their places at one of the tables;
Louise was seated at another and had beckoned
Cabot to take the chair beside her. Danielle saw
him shake his head, but he stood behind her at her
shoulder, apparently as absorbed in the play as she.

Carlos Diego frowned. 'I'd hoped Louise would
want to hold only a watching brief tonight,' he said.
'However—come and meet these friends of mine
who will want to talk to you about England. Unless
you'd rather play yourself?'

After a time he left her with the couple whom he
introduced. They spoke excellent English and
claimed they were anglophiles. More people joined
them and Danielle stayed long enough with the
group to decide she wouldn't be missed if she left.
She looked again for Carlos, but could not see him.
Cabot was still at Louise's elbow, from which she
would *not* collect him. She wandered a little aim-
lessly out of the casino alone, and almost bumped
into Felipe Diego leaving the bar.

'Hullo-ullo,' he greeted her familiarly. 'Alone?
Come and look at the moon from the balcony.'
His thick hand clasped her arm.

He had had two or three aperitifs before dinner,

wine at dinner, and had been in the bar since they had arrived at the club. Danielle thought it best to humour him, so she fell into step with him. 'Is there a moon?' she asked.

'If not, we'll order one.' They went out through a french window on to a stone-balustraded balcony looking out over the beach and the sea. There was no moon, and if there had been its light would have been dimmed by the white glare from the beach hotels, still in festive dress and mood long after midnight.

Felipe guided Danielle to lean on the balustrade. Elbow to elbow with her, 'Where is Louise?' he asked.

'At a roulette table,' she told him.

'And your fiancé?'

'Cabot? He was watching her play.'

'Leaving you alone?' Felipe shook his head in slow, heavy movement. There was a slurring of his 's' sounds as he added, 'You shouldn't allow this. Louise is a lovely woman. I adore her and she knows it. But she is a thief of men, and she will snatch yours if you do not guard him from her.'

The same measurement of Louise as Gina's! Louise the harpy, Cabot her marked-down prey. Was that the way it was—only that? Danielle wondered . . . hoped. Her own suspicions of an intrigue masterminded by Cabot, not by Louise, had waxed and waned so often that she scarcely knew what she herself currently believed.

She defended Cabot a little wearily. 'I've only been alone for a minute or two. I was with your brother when Cabot and Louise went to the tables.' She turned about. 'Shall we go back now?'

'Ah, not yet. What's wrong with my company? Tell me?' There was truculence in Felipe's tone.

'Nothing, of course. But——'

'Now that I've warned you, you want to call Cabot back to your side?' Felipe shook his head again. 'Now that would not be wise. Of all things, a man detests to be called to heel in public, like a puppy.'

'As if I *would* crook my finger at Cabot, expecting him to come running!' Danielle retorted irritably.

'No, much better that you make him come in search of *you*,' Felipe agreed thickly. 'Much better still for him to fear you could be occupied in much the same way yourself.'

She lost patience. 'In *what* same way?'

'With another man. Like this——' He swung her inward to face him, and though she braced back with her hands upon his chest, she was no match for the flabby weight of the man, and he drew her close.

His breath was heavy on her cheek as his lips sought hers, and though she jerked her head aside, they found the angle of her jaw and nuzzled sickeningly along it to her mouth, where they held and vainly probed her resistance. Why should one kiss so revolt, while another made rapture? she had time to wonder before she broke free, panting——

To find, as evidently Felipe had already realised, that they were not alone. Cabot was there, one hand on the balustrade, the other on his hip, with an air of waiting.

He addressed Felipe. 'When you are ready,' he said with a tinge of sarcasm, 'the Verdes are leaving and will drop you at Laura's if you don't want to wait for Carlos and for Louise, who doesn't want to leave the tables yet.'

Felipe pulled down his jacket and straightened his tie. 'I've had enough. I'll go with the Verdes,' he said.

'They're waiting.' When Felipe had left with a perfunctory bow to Danielle, Cabot turned to her.

'Would you like to play at the tables yourself? Or dance?' he invited.

If she had to face a grilling on this absurd scene with Felipe, the sooner the better. 'It's late. I'd rather go back to the yacht,' she said.

'Very well. While you fetch your wrap, I'll see Carlos for a moment, and call the car.'

Though their chauffeur was Portuguese and they were talking in English, they only discussed the dinner party and the evening on the journey back to the quay.

On board Cabot took her wrap from her and led the way to the lounge. Stooping to the drinks cabinet, 'A nightcap? What will you have?' he asked.

She didn't want a drink, but to have a glass in her hand might give her confidence for the inquisition to come. 'Just a tonic water, nothing in it,' she told him.

He excused himself to see if any radio calls had come in. He came back, reading some message slips. 'London is still a little excited about us, but our story seems to have gone across well so far,' he remarked. 'The columnist who claims to scoop all the rest has "inside information" that we mean to marry before we go back.' Thrusting the slips into a pocket, he poured himself a drink and sat down.

'I shall have a full day all tomorrow and shall need Simon. I think you should take Gina into Lisbon to see the city. Shall I order a guide for you, or would you rather explore by yourselves?' he asked.

'By ourselves, I think. I know what to look for, from the book you lent me.'

'You can have Jaime and the car. Let him drop you and pick you up wherever you like. Tomorrow will be our last full day in port. Louise and Felipe will come on board in time for sailing the evening after. Our next landfall, Tangier.'

So? No grilling, no third degree on Felipe's assault on her, giving her no chance to explain? Danielle, in fighting trim to rebut accusations, felt perversely cheated that they had not come. She made an opening herself. 'By the way,' she said, 'I think someone should have warned me that Felipe Diego gets rather—foolish when he's had too much to drink.'

'Perhaps one thought you had enough experience to recognise the signs,' Cabot returned coolly.

'Of his drinking? Of course I knew from his speech, but not until after we were on the balcony. He'd asked me to go to see the view, and I hope you don't suggest that, in going, I should have expected all that mauling and pawing from him? At only my second meeting with the man—Really!' Danielle snapped.

'*Were* you being pawed and mauled against your will?' Cabot insinuated. 'From where I was stand-ing——'

'You were mistaken!'

'In supposing that it was taking two to tango,

and that it was almost a pity to break it up?'

His complacency puzzled and enraged her. 'You thought that I was a party to it? That I wanted him to——? And if you did think that, don't you—care?'

Momentarily his lion-gold eyes flashed fire. 'Care? Why should I? To what depth?' he asked.

'Depth? At least to the depth, I'd have thought, of making some show of indignation.'

'Indignation against whom? You or Felipe?'

'Against us both, if you thought I was willing. I'm supposed to be engaged to you, aren't I? And if you believe me that he forced me, I'd expect you would want to ensure it didn't happen again.'

'Are you suggesting I should have demanded pistols for two at dawn or that I should forbid Diego to set foot on board on Wednesday?' Cabot queried.

'Well, you must realise, surely, that I'm going to be embarrassed by his being on board for the rest of the way?' Danielle pressed.

'Oh, come! You must have enough poise to rise above a caper he'll have forgotten by tomorrow! And if he was as far seas over as I judged him to be, he probably thought he was scoring with Louise anyway——'

Danielle pounced. 'But you'd have interfered for *her*?'

Cabot suppressed a yawn. 'Hypothetical question—it wasn't Louise's willingness being canvassed. It was yours.'

'Which makes it all right for me to "rise above it," I suppose?' she sneered.

'If I can, you can. And I certainly have no intention of dispensing with Felipe's business expertise on the trip, just because, being male, he's tempted to chance his arm with any attractive sex object that's handy.'

'I was *not* handy!'

'But you were there.'

She found a riposte to that. 'As, I suppose, I was "there" when you were tempted to try *your* arm?'

Cabot gestured towards her empty glass, and took it from her when she shook her head and stood up. He went with her to the door and along the corridor to her cabin, a hand lightly at her back. He chuckled shortly. 'My dear, that was no experimental foray. I was merely stating my rights!'

Over her shoulder she defied him. 'You have no rights over me.'

'My contractual rights, I meant. Neither of us lays claim to any of the emotional kind, do we?'

'No.'

'Then this needn't be misunderstood.' With one hand on the handle of her door, the other tilting her chin, he kissed her, dry-lipped and coolly, and stood back.

Stating your entire indifference to me—what I feel, what I am—she addressed him furiously from behind her closed door. And then, with devastating candour, asked herself, so what do you want of him *but* his indifference? And couldn't find any but a woolly, evasive answer to that.

CHAPTER FOUR

In planning the tour of Lisbon Cabot had reckoned without Gina's ideas on the matter. She joined Danielle at the car wearing a swimsuit under a thigh-brief skirt, and when they were some distance from the quay she said, 'Tell Jaime to drive to a beach somewhere, will you?'

'A beach?' Danielle echoed. 'But we're going into the city.'

'*You* may be, I'm not. Sightseeing, views, museums and things—no, thanks. I'm going to have a day sunbathing and swimming.' Gina tapped Jaime on the shoulder, gesturing to him to stop.

Danielle said, 'That wasn't at all the idea. If you could have the car again, you could go to a beach tomorrow before we sail.'

'I want to go today. So how about our splitting—you go into the city, and Jaime drives me to a beach—right?'

Danielle recognised Gina's stubborn mood. 'We can't do that. We must keep together,' she said.

'Why?'

'Because. Oh, all right,' Danielle gave in, 'tell Jaime what you want. He understands enough English for that.'

Jaime did. 'Beach? Estoril? Cascais?' he offered, and then with an effort, '*Hippy* beach?'

'Oh yes,' Gina clamoured, and turned to

Danielle. 'There'll be some kids there, and some music!'

Though not too many and not too much, was Danielle's pious prayer, which was answered when Jaime drove them to a secluded sandy cove where only half a dozen or so scantily clad teenagers were playing around, and the only musical instrument was a harmonica, the tinny strains of which were borne away on the breeze.

Gina was greeted without reserves at once and presently she was playing in the sea with the others, two of whom, a boy and a girl, were American holidaymakers. She came back to flop beside Danielle, who had stripped off as far as she decently could to sunbathe.

'When I asked why I shouldn't do my thing and you should do yours, what did you mean when you said "Because"?' Gina demanded.

'Just that it wasn't worth explaining why it wasn't on,' Danielle told her.

'Meaning Cabot has made you promise to stick to me like a leech? That makes you into a bit of a governess type, doesn't it?'

'Does it?'

'Then he *has* told you to see I don't get away!' Gina crowed. 'And I wouldn't put it past you both to be in league with my mother about that.'

'You must know I've never met your mother, and all I know from Cabot is that she lives in Monte Carlo and is waiting for you to join her there.'

'My, he's pretty cagey with you, isn't he?' (Danielle reflected that Louise Diego had made much the same incredulous comment. As his fiancée, she ought to know more than Cabot had told her.) 'Mean to say he hasn't told you Mother is planning to marry me off for money pretty well as soon as she gets me there?' Gina continued.

'Cabot didn't tell me so, but Louise Diego did,' Danielle admitted.

Gina grunted. 'Shows how close she keeps to him. She must have heard it from him. I suppose she'll be smarming phoney sympathy over me all the way from here to the Riviera. Not that I don't need someone to care a bit. But not *her*.' Grinding a blade of dune-grass in her teeth, Gina sat up, cross-legged, and waved a hand towards her morning's companions. 'Look at them,' she demanded. '*They're* going back to school or to college or to train for jobs—all of them around my age. Why should I be the one to be—be *sold*?'

Danielle protested, 'Gina, what a word to use—sold!'

Gina turned on her. 'Well, what else is it, you tell me? Dad was going to divorce Mother, but he died before he did. He left me five hundred pounds; everything else he had, which wasn't much, went to her, and she needs a lot of money. So she says she can't afford to keep me at school any longer, and plans to turn me into a kind of asset instead, by grooming me for marriage with one of her rich friends. She sits there in this Monte Carlo apartment, choosing a suitable victim like a—a spider in its web——'

'Shut up!' Danielle cut in peremptorily. 'She is your *mother*, and you make her sound like a monster!'

'Well——?'

'Which she can't be. She couldn't be plotting like this against you.'

'Or your dear, dear Cabot wouldn't be a party to handing me over to her?' Gina sneered.

'Well, would he? Would anyone? And he is your godfather, isn't he?'

'That doesn't mean a thing. He was only Dad's cousin, and he must have taken me on when he wasn't much older than I am now.'

'He's offering you a trip now which a lot of people of your age would give their ears for, and which I know he wanted you to enjoy,' Danielle reminded.

'The condemned man's hearty breakfast?'

'Don't dramatise!' Danielle snapped, and then, 'Look, may I talk to Cabot about this, and see what he says?'

Gina knelt up on the sand. 'Talk away. What can he say, but that I'm telling the truth?'

'We'll see, and I'll report back,' Danielle promised.

'O.K.' As Gina stood and made to go back to her friends, she warned over her shoulder, 'But meanwhile, don't try to police me, either of you— or you could be sorry!'

They all lunched together in a party including Jaime, at a little bar behind the beach. The menu was fresh sardines fried in butter, with crusty bread and the local red wine. Afterwards they all took a siesta on the sands before they parted.

Gina still did not want to 'do' the city, so she and Danielle returned in late afternoon to the yacht. Gina went to her cabin and Danielle, on her

way to her own, was surprised to meet Louise on
that deck.

Louise feigned guilt. 'Oh dear, caught more or
less in the act!' she simpered. 'I've been lunching
with Cabot—you mustn't mind. He suggested last
night that I might like to see my quarters, so I
drove over, not knowing of course that he'd sent
you and Gina on a sightseeing tour. I was sorry to
miss you, but he made the best of having to
entertain me and—but I suppose you know?—
he's giving me the state suite on C deck, the
generous man!'

Danielle said, 'Yes, I did know. I hope you'll be
comfortable there.'

'How could I *not* be? Of course I told him I
thought it should be reserved in case he ever enter-
tains people like the Monaco Royals or any Greek
millionaires, and that if anyone had it, *you* should.
But when I saw where you are—next door to him—
naturally I didn't argue any more. I had literally to
send him back to his office after luncheon, telling
him I'd see myself ashore, and I'm leaving now.
Did you have a good day?' Louise concluded without waiting with any interest for Danielle's reply.

Danielle went on to her own cabin. While she
bathed and changed for the evening, she wondered
wryly how much practice the Louise Diegos of this
world needed in order to plant their verbal barbs
with such telling accuracy. Louise *hadn't* been sorry
to find she could lunch alone with Cabot; she *had*
managed to imply that Cabot had arranged it so,
and her coy hints about the convenience of Cabot's
adjacent cabin to Danielle's own had been adroitly
chosen.

Danielle decided Gina certainly had something in her dislike of Louise.

Cabot came to the sundeck for drinks an hour later, before Gina or Simon appeared.

'Louise invited herself to lunch,' was his version. 'She claimed to be pleased with her suite.'

'Yes, so she said. I met her as she was leaving,' Danielle replied.

'And your own day—how did that go?'

Danielle laughed. 'I'm afraid that was a non-event. Gina and I know about as much about the sights of Lisbon as we did this morning. We spent the day at a hippie beach instead.'

'At a *beach*? Where? Why?'

'I don't really know where. Jaime was our guide, and it wasn't so very hippie—just a few teenagers doing their own thing. As to why—Gina flatly refused to be force-fed with culture, so I was diplomatic about it and let her have her way.'

Cabot frowned. 'That was more than she deserved. You'd have liked to see the city yourself?'

'After what I've read about it, yes. But I enjoyed the day all the same.'

'All the same,' Cabot echoed, 'you should have seen Lisbon while you had the chance.'

'Well, I've lost it now. I've promised both the chefs I'll check their share of the stores tomorrow, and there are the Diegos' cabins to get ready.'

'And I must be on board all day. And so,' Cabot drained the drink he had poured for himself, 'that leaves only tonight, so we'll dispense with Jaime and drive in together after dinner. Or no, we'll dine in the city, and though the public places will be shut, we can drive around it and up into the hills.'

Danielle wondered uncharitably for whose benefit was this exhibition of cordiality towards her,
but she took it at its face value and said, 'I'd like
that. Were you thinking of taking Gina too?'

'Pressganging her? No fear. She and Simon can
entertain each other again. Socially they're both
pretty gauche, and it will do them good. Besides,
so far we've provided our public with precious few
records of our shared experiences, and this will
make one for the book,' said Cabot, destroying any
illusion she might have been harbouring that he
had invited her for the sole enjoyment of her company.

The dark southern night was still warm when
they set out, the streets and shops of the inner city
still brilliantly lit and attracting the parading
crowds, and every seat under the trees of the outer
avenues and boulevards filled to capacity.

'One sees why the Latins furnish their houses so
sparsely. They can spend so much time out of doors
that they don't need furniture for comfort and
warmth as we do—simply for bare use,' Cabot
remarked at one point, and at another questioned
how many of the exquisite façades they passed on
the avenues would bear inspection of the deeper
structures behind them.

That touched a raw nerve in Danielle. 'That's
the property developer talking,' she challenged
him. 'Those lovely houses are *standing*, aren't they?
And probably have been for two or three centuries.
But you people have only to find flaws in their
cellars or whatever, and you'll have them down in
favour of blocks of flats!'

Her outburst appeared to surprise Cabot. He

threw her a glance. 'Oh, come,' he urged, 'we don't buy or sell in order to raze to the ground regardless. We employ architects to restore wherever it's feasible and safe.'

Danielle thought of the Terrace Adelaide, that gem of bow-fronted architecture to which she hadn't allowed herself to return after her aunt's death. 'You still raze too much,' she said.

'In your opinion, or of your expert knowledge?'

'Only in my opinion, of course.'

'Exactly,' he countered cruelly. 'And though I ought to force you to quote six examples of buildings which people like myself could have saved, for the sake of the rest of our evening, I won't. You're out of your depth on this subject, my dear, so let's leave it there, shall we?'

She left it. Though she longed to retort that she could quote just *one* example which could make a case for him to answer, she refrained. She was not ready yet—she hadn't enough proof—for creating a situation which would precipitate a showdown between them. She had been goaded into saying almost too much tonight, and after all, it had been she, not he, who had introduced the sour note into their talk. She managed a smile. 'Very well, let's leave it,' she said.

They were driving down one side of the magnificent, flower-emblazoned Avenida da Liberdade when he asked where they should dine. 'At one of the show places, or look for some local colour in a side-street *bodega*?'

'There, I think. I'm not dressed for dining in the grand manner,' she said.

The place to which he took her was a genuine

wine-cellar with foot-thick walls, stone floors, lantern-lit, and the few tables for patrons flanked by immense casks of maturing wine. Cabot and Danielle were the only foreigners in a chattering crowd of Portuguese.

Obviously the wine was the speciality of the house; the food, offered on a no-choice basis, was a *garbanzo* soup, like thick gruel, and trout, casseroled with herbs and wine and coated with cream. A dish of fresh fruit was the only dessert.

During the meal Danielle remembered her promise to Gina. She told Cabot, 'You suggested that Gina must tell me herself what her problems were, and today I think she did. She told me that she's being shipped to Monte Carlo, so that her mother can make a rich match for her. Considering her age, I found that unbelievable, but how much truth is there in it?'

'Some,' Cabot admitted. 'Exaggerated to impress you, of course, but I know Beatrix Lisle is casting about on those lines—seeing Gina as an asset she might realise.'

'But that's barbaric, if it's true! Can you wonder that Gina's embittered? If Mrs Lisle needs to scheme for money, why doesn't she make a rich second marriage herself, instead of sacrificing Gina?'

Cabot shrugged. 'Probably opportunity would be a fine thing. Beatrix is in her mid-forties, and to men of a certain type Gina's mere youth could have an appeal which Beatrix knows she hasn't any longer—or more likely, knows she hasn't while she must own to a going-on-seventeen-year-old daughter. If she can marry Gina off to anyone at all, she might pass for thirty herself, and be free to do her own fortune-hunting.'

'And knowing this about Mrs Lisle, you're prepared to stand by and let it all happen to Gina?'

'Gina is merely my godchild; I'm in no legal relationship to either of them. So yes, I'm prepared to take her to her mother, and nothing particularly dire has happened to her yet. Nor, I'd say, is anything in the way of marriage likely to come her *way*, while she has as little of the poise and grooming which—' in his pause Cabot's eyes travelled purposefully over Danielle—'I'd hoped she might learn from you.'

'In just a few weeks, even if people of her age saw anything worth imitating in people of mine?' Danielle scoffed. 'There's a gap between us the width of the Cheddar Gorge, and she lumps you and me together as policemen she wouldn't hesitate to defy if we stepped out of line.'

'Been uttering threats, has she?'

Danielle hesitated. 'Perhaps only blustering, but she sounded as if she meant that we'd be sorry if we tried to pull rank on her too much.'

'Why, what could she do? Jump ship and hitch-hike her way back to England? *She* would be the one to be sorry if she tried it.'

'And that,' retorted Danielle, 'is the kind of threat which could tempt her to try it. I promised her I'd ask you to confirm or deny what she'd told me about her mother, and as you've more or less confirmed it, what can I tell her to reassure her now?'

'I doubt if she genuinely wants reassuring at the moment. While no one can contradict her she's getting a kick out of persuading you and Simon Milward, and anyone who'll listen, that she's a helpless martyr to her mother's plans. To tell her that her fears are groundless would be to cut the ground from beneath her aggrieved feet.'

'Simon?' Danielle questioned. 'Has she confided in him too?'

'Oh yes. He's already as indignant for her as you are, seeing himself as her knight in shining armour. But you're both wasting your sympathy while she's thriving on it, and it seems a pity to spoil her fun,' Cabot drawled.

Danielle was silent for a moment. Then, 'Are you always as cynical as this? Or do you reserve your doubts of people for specially selected targets?' she asked.

The tawny eyes widened. 'Cynical? Now *that's* an accusation I insist you justify with examples— come!'

He was baiting her and enjoying it, and she knew it. She hesitated. 'It's not fair to expect me to quote, off the cuff. But you prejudge people. You claim to know their motives are phoney, when they may not be. You're judging Gina like that now. You've judged *me*. For instance——'

'Ah, an example at last!' he mocked. 'Let's have it.'

'Well—last night I know you'd decided I'd encouraged Felipe Diego, and though you pretended to believe I hadn't, your whole attitude was shouting that you didn't,' she accused.

'Why, I gave you the benefit of the doubt, didn't I?'

'Cynically. Boredly. Implying that I was working myself up over nothing.'

Cabot sighed. 'Oh dear, we're back at my lack of concern, are we? At my refusal to have Felipe horsewhipped for getting amorous in his cups? Cynical of me, that—to recognise his besotted advances as occupational hazards of your sex appeal, of no consequence at all, except to your outraged self-esteem?'

'Just one of those tipsy male nonsenses you'd expect me to be able to ride, I suppose?' Danielle picked up her bag and he came round the table to draw out her chair for her.

'If you didn't welcome them, I'd judge you capable of it, yes,' he said.

'If I didn't welcome them!' she exploded. But he only laughed and took her arm.

'All right,' he said, 'I admit I was hoping you were going to slap the fellow's face. But you split before you did and I couldn't be sure you weren't co-operating.'

She supposed she must take that as his olive-branch, and for the moment she was glad to. He had given her no satisfaction over Gina's fears, but apart from their two brushes of argument, he had had the decency to give her a pleasant evening. But for his invitation she would have carried away very little impression of Lisbon.

He drove up into the hills for a birds-eye view of the city and the sea, and then drove back by a circuitous route to the yacht. He went with her to the door of her cabin, where she tensed to the possibility he might expect more from her than her thanks for the evening. If he did, what would she say . . . do? Of course she would rebuff him, but she could not deny a memory of her senses' treacherous excitement when he had exacted a toll of her lips once before. The man's expertise in making love without loving had been too much for her will against him, and might be again if she were weak enough to imply Yes in answer to a demand he might think he had a right to make.

To her relief—or was it an anti-climax?—he made none. His shrug dismissed her own murmured thanks, and after opening her door for her, he left her on the threshold with a perfunctory, 'Sleep as well as I mean to. We've a full day before us tomorrow,'—as prosaic a parting as she could have wished, though whether or not she had wanted it to be quite so detached she wasn't sure. She would have liked to hear he had enjoyed her company too. But that was to cut the hostile distance between them, which was a softening she must not afford.

Her last thoughts before she slept were of the evening, and some two hours later she was dreaming that someone who was Cabot, yet was not Cabot, in the crazy way of dreams, was taunting her efforts to escape from a maze, when she waked, bemused, to a knock on her door.

Her robe wasn't handy, and still half asleep, she padded barefoot to open, possibly to Gina, she supposed. But it was Cabot on the threshold, he too undressed. 'It's Gina—she's ill. Can you come?' he said crisply.

'Yes. Yes, of course.' As she reached for a gown and thrust her feet into mules the phantasy Cabot her dream had conjured turned into the Cabot of reality and she was fully awake. 'Ill? How do you know? What's the matter with her?' she asked.

She was struggling with a wide sleeve turned inside out, and with an impatient, 'Tch!' Cabot reached to adjust it. 'She's vomiting continually and says she thinks she fainted before she managed to ring for the night steward, who came to me. Ready now?' He went ahead along the corridor and down to the lower deck where the nervous boy stood, twisting his fingers, outside Gina's open door.

'All right, Suli. But don't go to bed,' Cabot dismissed him.

'He's new this trip; we're travelling light of an English medical orderly. Can you cope?' Cabot asked Danielle.

'I hope so.' She went to Gina sitting on the edge of her bed, head sunk into hands which were damp with sweat when Danielle touched them. 'Gina dear, what——?' she asked.

Gina looked up, ashen-faced, tears of strain filling her eyes. 'Awful,' she quavered. 'I've been so sick. I——Oh!' Clutching at Danielle for support, she staggered over to the fitted basin where nausea did its worst with her again. Shivering and spent, 'That's——better,' she managed, adding at the same moment as Danielle mentally diagnosed food poisoning, 'It must have been that wretched fish. Simon didn't have it, but I did——'

'*Fish*? Bad fish? Served to you at dinner?' Cabot cut in, looking a question at Danielle, who was smoothing the bed and helping Gina back into it, covering her over.

'Not on board. Fish wasn't on the menu tonight,' she told him, and then, 'Look, it's pretty obvious she's been poisoned by something—fish or whatever—she's eaten. But her colour's coming back and she could have got clear of it now. So perhaps you'd better leave us to it, and she may be able to get back to sleep. I'll stay with her until she does.'

'But where could——?'

Danielle, in authority over him as well as over Gina, snapped, 'Never mind that now. It can wait, and Gina isn't up to questions, so please go back to bed. We can get along without you—really.'

'Shall I call a doctor to her?'

Danielle shook her head. 'Not necessary at this hour. In the morning, perhaps.'

'Anything you want for her? Anything she ought to have?'

Danielle thought for a moment. 'No food, obviously. But yes—— If she's finished—performing, brandy could warm and settle her tum.'

Cabot nodded agreement. 'I'll send the boy with a tot.' At the door he paused. 'I shan't go to bed. I shall wait up,' he said. But he left Danielle with a small but gratifying sense of power—a very rare phenomenon indeed between Cabot Steele, tycoon, and Danielle Kane, his hired help!

Presently Gina, heartened by the brandy, was anxious to talk. 'It must have been that beastly fish,' she said again. 'It was my fault. I made Simon take me ashore. We hired a cab and told the man to drive us somewhere interesting. He took us miles, doing a running commentary in Portuguese that we didn't understand. I'd cancelled dinner aboard here, and when we asked him to take us to a restaurant, he chose a low-down joint in a back street which he managed enough English to say it had "much glamour". Simon turned up his nose, but I was hungry, and there was this fishy concoction swimming in oil but smelling marvellous, which I had but he didn't. The "glamour" didn't hit me until I'd been in bed an hour, but then did it! I'll say it did!'

Danielle said, 'I ought to tell you it served you right for not choosing a decent restaurant for yourselves. What could Simon be thinking of? This second-rate place probably gave your man a commission on the customers he brought. Anyway, Cabot isn't going to be too pleased that you left the yacht at night without his permission. He's responsible for you on this trip, you know.'

'Well, he needn't give Simon a thick ear about it. *I* persuaded him we had a right to go, considering how you'd swanned off two nights running, leaving us to whoop it up over a quiet game of Ludo. And I daresay it will be the same in every port we make; you'll put the children to bed before you go out on the town,' Gina claimed sulkily.

'I promise you we won't, if *you'll* promise not to repeat tonight's caper,' said Danielle.

'I'm not promising. I could break it if I get too bored,' was all Gina would allow, and Danielle decided against pushing the issue any further. Gina claimed to be more comfortable since taking the brandy, but she did not sleep for a long time, and when at last she did, Danielle stayed at her bedside for most of another hour. By which time it was nearly dawn, and full of needed sleep herself, she returned to her cabin, to find Cabot in residence there.

He was sitting, asleep with his head supported on his hand. He had not heard her arrival, and she stood for a minute or two, looking at him and feeling even for him the compassion due to the defencelessness of sleep . . . feeling also a strangely compulsive desire to watch him unawares, his fine head drooped, his bronzed bare torso from which the loosened waist-sash had allowed his gown to fall away, his unconscious figure relaxed and vulnerable.

She felt an inexplicable urge to wake him by smoothing the ruffled auburn hair—— But what was she thinking of? Asleep or awake, he was who he was, and they were as remote from each other as the far stars.

He came to, stretching, his eyes focusing on her, and he stood. He pointed to her bedside clock. 'It's almost morning,' he said. 'Have you been with Gina all this time?'

Danielle sat down on her bed, suddenly longing to get into it. 'Yes. She took ages to go off to sleep, but she's through the worst of it now,' she told him.

'But this fish she thinks was bad—how did she come by it? We left her and Milward to dine together!'

'Yes, but they didn't eat on board,' Danielle explained a little wearily. 'She took umbrage at not being invited ashore on two nights, and she more or less bullied Simon into taking her round the town by taxi.' Danielle watched the hard set of Cabot's mouth as he listened.

'Simon had no right to let her bully him,' he

said. 'He's going to hear about that from me!'

'Yes, well—if he hadn't agreed to go with her, I wouldn't put it past Gina to go alone—her idea of taking it out on us for ducking our duty to keep her amused,' Danielle pointed out.

'On which supposed duty I shall have a few words to say when she's better,' Cabot promised grimly. 'I'm taking her to Monte Carlo as a favour; as far as she knows, you and I are engaged, and if she supposes she can tag along whenever I choose to take you out, she'd better think again. Anyway, where did she get this fish?'

'She let the taxi-driver show them to some low dive to eat, and she fell to with gusto, overruling Simon again.'

'He didn't eat the stuff? He's all right?'

'Apparently.' Danielle leaned back on her hands, outspread behind her on the bed, head thrown back, she sighed deeply, murmured, 'Oh, I'm tired,' almost to herself, then sat up abruptly as she caught Cabot's gaze at her pose, lest he thought she had made it deliberately provocative.

He looked away indifferently. 'No wonder,' he said, came to her and stooped to tap each of her shins in turn, in the way of a farrier persuading a mare to lift a hoof for inspection. He removed her mules, then taking her legs bodily, straightened her on the bed, shook up her pillows and drew the single sheet over her.

He stood for a moment looking down at her before he bent, supporting himself by his fists on either side of her body, and kissed her gently on the mouth.

'No dastardly assault intended—merely in the

cause of goodwill,' he told her start of surprise as he switched off the light and went out. She was glad he could not know that if she had expected the kiss her lips might have parted in invitation— but only at the same strange impulse which had wanted to touch his hair; nothing at all to do with any surrender to his will.

CHAPTER FIVE

LOUISE, met on deck by Danielle and followed up the gangway by Felipe, looked as if she doubted her hearing.

'Such a disappointment,' she murmured. 'And such a nuisance, having to live out of one's suitcase while—Are you *sure* Cabot wanted me to give up the state suite to Gina? Or did you arrange it yourself?' she demanded of Danielle, who explained a second time.

'No, they were Cabot's orders. You see, the state suite is the only one with twin rooms, opening out of each other, and he thought it best I should sleep there for one night with Gina. He felt sure you wouldn't mind using her cabin instead. It's small, but I've had her things moved out of it, and it's all ready for you, and Senhor Diego's is ready for him.'

Louise's shrug and grimace were ungracious. 'Oh well, I suppose—as it won't be for long,' she allowed. 'Let's hope Gina has been taught a lesson. Where is it—her cabin? And Felipe's?

'The deck below this. The steward will show you.' Danielle clapped to summon the boy. 'If you need anything, tell him, won't you?' As she watched Felipe, weighed down by Louise's hand luggage as well his own, follow down the short companionway, Danielle wondered what Louise would say when she found there was no en-suite bath to Gina's cabin.

Gina had been fully recovered by the morning, but Cabot had been firm that Danielle should be within close call for another night. Gina's comment, not made in his hearing, was that Louise would surely have preferred Danielle's empty cabin, which handily shared a bathroom with his, as well as a connecting door.

As from Southampton, *Pandora* sailed in the early evening, slipping out from the Tagus on a smooth tide. Once out at sea the next sight of land would be Cape St Vincent on the horizon, with then some forty hours' sailing to the Straits of Gibraltar and Tangier.

Danielle, busy all day, had not heard what Cabot had said either to Gina or to Simon about the Lisbon escapade, but later, to Danielle, Simon chivalrously took the blame for it, complaining only, 'It's the devil's own job, arguing with Gina. If she's decided yes, she might never have heard of no.'

That evening they dined without Gina, who elected to go to bed early with her dinner on a tray, not, Danielle suspected, because she was still convalescent, but because she couldn't bring herself to the courtesy of thanking Louise for giving up her suite.

In face of Cabot's orders, Louise hadn't had any choice, had she? she argued. You *bet* she wouldn't have offered of her own free will!

After dinner their party split up. Cabot and Felipe talked business, Simon went to the library to watch television and Danielle was again the subject of Louise's probing curiosity.

Since *Pandora* had arrived in Lisbon, the English

papers had come in, their gossip columns *full* of Cabot's escape with his fiancée, said Louise. Why *had* he made such a mystery of his engagement to Danielle; how long they had known each other and so on? Louise wanted to know. Hadn't he learned by now that in business all publicity was good, even when it was critical? But by any chance, *could* the newshounds think they knew something—well, spicy, perhaps, about Danielle's past? No, of course there needn't *be* anything—Louise answered her own question. But really, Cabot hadn't helped matters by being so cagey!

Danielle, fencing desperately, tried to turn the conversation to other things. After being forced to the evasion that she knew of nothing shady about the engagement on which the columnists could batten, she hoped to steer Louise in a less dangerous direction by asking her whether she knew Tangier.

Vain hope. Surprisingly Louise did not. But Danielle did? Really? When had she been there? With whom? To which Danielle was sorely tempted to reply, 'I was keeping an assignation with my Arab lover,' but she refrained, and told instead the prosaic truth that she had spent a week there on a package tour two years earlier.

When the men rejoined them later Louise switched off her interest in Danielle, turning it instead upon Cabot.

'A fine host you are!' she taunted him archly. 'My first night aboard, and, except at dinner you've been practically invisible!' She looked round the big saloon. 'Do you ever dance here? Why don't we?'

'If you like.' Cabot moved to the music centre and she went with him. 'What do you want? Disco-jerking? Old time?' he asked.

'Oh, something romantic, cheek-to-cheek dreamy,' she claimed. 'I feel sentimental tonight.' As she hummed a few bars of the nostalgic waltz which Cabot selected, Felipe moved over to her, arms invitingly open. But she waved him back. 'No, I can dance with you any time. I'm going to be terribly mean to Danielle and——' without finishing the sentence she went to Cabot and slinked into his hold.

A sheepish Felipe returned to Danielle. 'Take pity on me?' he invited, and irked by Louise's blatant rebuff of him, she said brightly, 'Why not? I'm a lone wolf too.'

His dancing was elephantine, but she was determined to bear with it for as long as Louise monopolised Cabot. Beyond Felipe's shoulder she watched the other two. Louise had made the advance, but wasn't Cabot co-operating enthusiastically too? She hoped he would note how readily she had risen above her aversion to Felipe when he had capitulated to Louise!

Cabot had said Felipe would forget his drunken approaches at La Bella Mar, but he hadn't. He took credit for them. 'You see, I was right,' he told Danielle as they danced. 'You needed to show Cabot how desirable you are to other men, and I helped you to do it. If I hadn't made him jealous for you, he wouldn't have tried to snub me as he did. As I remember telling you, it's the only way to snatch a man back from a woman with the charm of Louise. And——' he drew her closer—'you seem to have learned your lesson. You are being specially nice to me!'

For the second time that evening Danielle held her tongue. She was dying to point out icily that when he had forced himself upon her, he couldn't have known Cabot would be there to mistake her recoil for a willingness of which he could be jealous. But diplomacy held her back. Cabot would claim that keeping his guests happy for their business value to him was partly what he paid her for, and though it might be craven of her to obey him to the letter, she supposed she must try.

She bore with Felipe for as long as she thought she need—whereupon Louise made a show of guilt for having annexed Cabot, and scolded Danielle for letting her get away with it. 'Though you may have to learn, my dear,' she whispered, 'that other women with fewer scruples than I have are going to find your Cabot irresistible. Make him dance with you now—oh!' She broke off as Cabot came up behind Danielle and with both hands at her waist, turned her about and into his arms.

He danced, as she was coming to learn he did most things, with assured ease, giving the impression that that particular skill was effortless. He brought the same careless confidence to their own intrigue. So far she couldn't fault his public manner with her, seeming to be ridden by none of her own misgivings. He had assumed with an unfailing instinct the way of an engaged man with his chosen woman—with reined-in ardour, and courtesy and a cajoling tenderness. He might almost be counting her as really his fiancée ... Which—Danielle brought up her thoughts with a jerk—was impossible and absurd.

He was putting on an act now, for the benefit of Felipe and Louise—touching her hair with his lips, drawing her close, aligning the curve of her body to his, holding her off to look with meaning promise into her eyes. She would have liked a man she loved to look at her like that; she would understand the promise and enjoy it. But he was only showing off. He didn't mean it. She couldn't have wanted him to . . . could she?

When at last he released her, Louise had lost interest in dancing and said so. Cabot switched off the music, Simon came in and they had a final drink before parting for the night.

Gina was asleep and remained so while Danielle undressed in her own room of the suite. Gina's door was slightly ajar, and she left hers the same when she got into bed and prepared to read. She was not sleepy, and she read on until she suddenly remembered she had gone back to her own cabin to fetch something before dressing for the evening, and had left her wrist watch in the bathroom there. It was precious to her, her father's engagement present to her mother, and she always liked to wear it at night as her mother had done. There was no sound from Gina; she could slip up and get it within minutes, and that without bothering with slippers or gown.

By the dim light in the deck corridor she saw the door to her empty cabin was open. She went through it and through the connecting door to the bathroom. She didn't need a light; she knew just where she had left the watch and felt for it. It was not there.

She caught a breath of dismay. This *was* where——! She fumbled along the shelf in vain, and was about to reach for the light switch when she heard movement from Cabot's adjoining master cabin. She stayed where she was in the dark as his door opened and Louise emerged into the shaft of light from the room. Her magnificent hair was loose on her shoulders and she was clutching the floating silk of a négligé about her. She looked back, giggling conspiratorially and turning the two fingers at her lips into a blown kiss before she pattered away.

Cabot's door closed. Shocked and irate, Danielle abandoned her search, waited until Louise must have reached her cabin, then went back to her own.

She sat on the edge of her bed, working on her surprise and anger. That Cabot should *dare* to risk sabotaging his own scheme by starting—or continuing?—an affair with Louise, one of the people it should have deceived!

He had claimed it was to preserve the proprieties, to ease Gina's acceptance of Danielle's escort, and to protect Danielle's own name from gossip. And all the while—*all the while* its object must have been the sheltering of Senhora Louise Diego from gossip! Louise, travelling without her husband, but with a brother-in-law who was her slave and with another man with whom, on her own boastful admission, she had had a liaison before her marriage—it was she who had to be provided with the 'cover' of that man's supposed fiancée and hostess, and further hedged about by such extra fellow travellers as Gina and Simon Milward.

Danielle thought back to how she had been almost persuaded to Gina's suggestion that Cabot needed 'cover' for an affair with Louise. At the time she had rejected it as unbelievably fantastic, but she had wondered later and was wondering now. No, more than wondering. Their assignation in his room surely proved it? And how could she— Danielle agonised with humiliation—how *could* she have allowed him to dupe her so?

Well, enough was enough. There was always tomorrow and a showdown he was not going to escape.

In the morning she did not mention the loss of her watch or her search for it to Gina. But she waylaid the night steward who told her, yes, the Mem had left it in her bathroom. He had found it and given it to 'him Sahib,' who had said he would see that the Mem got it. 'Good? All right?' the boy asked anxiously.

So Cabot had it. But Danielle made herself wait for him to tell her so. The showdown had to have an opening, and he should make it.

It was his habit after breakfast to study the news tapes and radio messages which had come in overnight, on the sundeck, and he invited her there, saying he had the watch for her.

'Thank you.' She took it from him. 'Suli told me he'd found it and given it to you. When was that?'

'When I was changing for the evening.'

'Well, I hadn't missed it by then. But why didn't you give it to me at dinner?'

He was looking at her with something near amusement. 'You'd said you liked to wear it through the night, so perhaps I was hoping you'd remember where you'd left it and would come to find it when you were ready for bed. Too bad you didn't. We could have——'

She flared at the mockery in his tone. 'But I did,' she retorted. 'Not as soon as I was in bed, but later. *Some time later*,' she emphasised, holding his glance.

She saw that he had understood. He laughed. 'Really? What astute timing! Was your visit really by accident? Or had you been listening at keyholes or decoding the Secret Plans? Though what a pity you didn't arrive a little earlier. We could have made a threesome party of it. It's said they're the best——'

At that she hit him, and had the satisfaction of seeing his flinch and the marks of her fingers on his cheek before her wrist was in a vice and there was neither amusement nor mockery in his eyes.

'Fisticuffs, eh? They'll get you nowhere,' he rasped.

'Nor will insults!' she panted. 'I was there in all ignorance, in search of my watch. How dare you assume I was spying on Louise, or that I'd be a party to your—your filthy suggestion? And what becomes of our pretence engagement now? What's it in aid of? What was it *ever* in aid of? Your lie that it was to avoid the tongue-wagging about your bringing me on the trip for Gina's sake and because you needed a hostess who wasn't a battleaxe? Or as a blanket for your affair with a woman whose name must be protected because she has a husband who's your friend and your business associate? Which?' Danielle's vehemence surprised and shocked even herself, and was in humiliating contrast to the icy calm with which Cabot heard her out.

As if in reproof to a child, he said, 'Since you seem convinced you know the truth, perhaps you'll tell *me* which you think it was?'

'You hoodwinked me, and I believed you,' she muttered.

'So you've decided which? Well, suppose you bring a little reason to bear on that? You come by chance on Louise in a foolish piece of mischief, and you immediately jump to conclusions of the worst. In fact, jump as passionately to conclusions as if you had the usual cause for jealousy of Louise—ludicrous idea! But just as ludicrous—do you really suppose I'd have to brew myself an elaborate alibi if I wanted an affair with Louise? *Or* would conduct it in my own yacht, in full view of my goddaughter and my business pupil, not to mention her husband's brother? Come on, be the intelligent age I hoped you were!' Cabot urged.

'Is it so unlikely, on the evidence? You'd invited her to your cabin at night!' Danielle retorted.

'I did *not* invite her.'

'You must have let her suppose she'd be welcome if she went there.'

Cabot's gesture was impatient. 'My dear judge and juror, a woman of Louise's sexuality doesn't question a man's welcome of her. If it isn't there at the outset, she's confident she can conjure it up.'

'As she did, considering the gaiety with which she was parting from you when I came on the scene,' Danielle said tartly. 'You don't expect me to believe you'd thrown her out?'

Cabot seemed to ponder that. Then he said

slowly, 'Do you know, I can't think it important what you believe about Louise's call on me? It's none of your business, and it's altered nothing in our agreed relationship—yours and mine.'

'Altered nothing? It has—has exploded it!'

'Nothing of the sort.'

'Well, it has for me. I thought it would give you some valuable business time, and would help you with Gina, and would spare *me* some gossip. Certainly not that you'd use it to save any suspicion of your being Louise Diego's lover. I supposed she was simply your guest, and that she believed we were engaged, and how do you imagine we can meet normally now, knowing what each of us knows?' Danielle demanded.

'Why not? All that Louise knows about you she knew before last night, and she knows no more now.'

'How can I believe that?'

'Because I tell you so—though under no obligation.'

'But that makes it all the worse! That way, she'll have got a kick from being one up on an engaged girl, and she'll have *enjoyed* it!' Danielle accused wildly.

Cabot said patiently, 'You can't have it both ways. Either you prefer Louise to know the truth or you don't. And since she doesn't, why waste your compassion on a fictitious fiancée who can be neither hurt nor jealous? Though from your righteous indignation, one could almost suppose you to be both.'

'That—that's ridiculous!'

'My error. However, I repeat—last night's tiresome incident has made no new difficulties for the insurance I bought with our pact, and for Louise it would have been no more than a thumb-to-the-nose to convention—a silly opener to the fun she's promised herself this trip. And so, with no harm done, what are we arguing about?'

'About me,' said Danielle. 'About a role I was able to act to, while I thought I hadn't to doubt your reasons for it——'

'You haven't to doubt them now.'

She sighed. 'I'm sorry. I don't want to. But you must see that after this, I can't pretend in front of Louise any more? For instance, if she sees you kiss me, she can savour it as a private joke——' Danielle drew her shoulders together in a shudder of distaste '*No!*'

Cabot moved over to the rail to lean nonchalantly against it. 'So, if you can't face an imaginary embarrassment with Louise, let's have it straight—what do you propose to do?' he asked.

'I'd ask you to release me from our agreement, and I'd leave the yacht at Tangier, I suppose.'

'You suppose? You've worked it out? Well, you could leave for Tangier today if you liked—*if* you could navigate the launch for a hundred miles or so, and *if* I would let you go.'

She stared across at him. 'You couldn't bind me to the agreement against my will!' But she feared he could.

'No? Well, until I decide the time has come to end it—try me,' he invited.

'I could sue you for—for breach of contract!' she almost shrilled.

'Of a contract *you'd* be breaking, but which I

can be seen to have honoured with every penny and gift and loverlike attention it promised you? Oh no, my dear.' He levered himself from the rail and came back to her. He pulled her to him to kiss her lightly and continued in a rough undertone, 'You haven't a legal leg to stand on, and if you did think of resorting to the courts for your release, I swear I'll take you for every asset you own. Understood?'

He left her without waiting for her reply—confident, she supposed, that his threats had spelled out her defeat.

But they hadn't. Beaten though she might be, it was for entirely other reasons that she would not be leaving *Pandora* at Tangier, nor dunning him publicly for a redress of her rights.

For one thing, her pride was rising to the challenge of proving that she was equal to Louise's intrigue. She would *show* Cabot.'

For another—as her indignation cooled, her thought veered to Gina, whom, if she broke with Cabot now, she would be abandoning to whatever fate awaited her at her mother's hands—a story which Danielle knew she couldn't influence, but which she didn't want to leave unfinished.

For yet another—back to Cabot now, and his firm's rape of the Terrace Adelaide—that unpaid score she still had stacked against him. If she cut loose from the cruise in Tangier there would be no future for that.

Dispassionately she mustered her reasons, added minor ones and decided she could stay without losing too much face. But she had to ignore the clamour of a small voice inside her that urged,

'Don't fool yourself, Danielle Kane. You're staying because you can't defy Cabot Steele. You're committed to him; he's fastened a magnet to you. If you could get away, you wouldn't go, and you don't have to hint for reasons why not. In your heart you don't want to leave him.'

In her *heart*?

Pandora docked at Tangier in mid-morning. From the sea the view of the city was a panorama of plaster walls, flat roofs, domed mosques, and towering minarets and Western skyscrapers dwarfing all. The bay itself was a great arc of golden sands, fronting a wide boulevard bordered by palms and breaking out into gardens at its European end, but dwindling and cheapening for as far as it skirted the long curved arm of the harbour wall that reached out to the east-pointing horn of the bay. Behind it the clutter and freight-rails of the quays had as background the piled mass of the blind walls of the Moorish quarter, secret and withdrawn.

Awaiting *Pandora*'s berthing there was a hired car to take her guests into the city, where the streets of the European quarter were a fascinating mixture of East and West.

The elegant shops, the couturiers, the cafés, the perfumeries, mostly traded under European names, but they had for patrons as many veiled women and Moroccan men as they had Western tourists and businessmen, and at that fashionable hour of the morning all social Tangier seemed to be living out of doors at street bars and pavement cafés and greeting its friends.

Sipping mint tea and nibbling almond tartlets on the roof terrace of a hotel with a view of the outline of the Spanish coast, Louise pronounced that Tangier was definitely her scene, and Cabot must realise she would refuse to leave it until she had drained its delights to the dregs.

She could gamble here? And go to a bullfight— Spanish style, not Portuguese, where the bull wasn't killed? For her daytime amusement there were these fabulous shops, and after dark Cabot must know of some scandalous all-night clubs. He must make up some parties to include some of these gorgeous Moors, for surely he knew some to invite.

During the days that followed Gina discovered and temporarily adopted a colony of kittens living wild on the perimeter of an Embassy garden, and spent her morning hours feeding buns to the patient hobbled donkeys and mules in the medina market-place. 'Might as well suck up to the four-footeds,' she grumbled to Danielle. 'These Moors are a lot of cissies who've been told they've got bedroom eyes, and if anything a bit more macho heaves on the horizon he goes down to Louise like a ninepin. Give me dumb animals every time!'

Simon was professionally attracted by the primitive architecture of old Tangier, its mazes of cobbled and mud-dried narrow alleys, its tall windowless houses looking inward only to domestic courtyards, their outer walls totally blank but for the occasional heavy studded door which appeared to have been barred for years. He filled a sketch block with impressionist watercolours and scale diagrams, and usually went off on this ploy when he had time off from his work for Cabot.

Felipe emerged as having more purpose than as Louise's minion. The brothers Diego had timber and cork contacts, mostly in Moorish hands, for which Felipe acted as linkman with Cabot Steele interests, and he was able to promote as many introductions to 'gorgeous Moors' as even Louise could crave.

Danielle, who had been wholly fascinated with the colourful facets of Moroccan life on her first visit, felt she was renewing a friendship with Tangier, making it her pleasure to walk its boulevards, explore the dingier passageways of the medina, and barter for flowers and trinkets and handwoven cloth and brassware at its market stalls.

Cabot had surprised her by having not once questioned her threat to leave the yacht. Without asking her, he could not have known whether or not she would defy him, but though she was irked by his bland assumption that she dared not, at least it spared her the humiliation of a surrender in so many words. She was more mortified at the thought of Louise's secret triumph in having, as she believed, poached the rights of Cabot's fiancée. They were the kind of illicit prize, Danielle suspected, that Louise would value, and Danielle longed to be able to tell her that between Cabot and herself, they did not exist. She had no rights, where Cabot was concerned, but those of a hired servant, and there might be a rag of perverse satisfaction to be wrung from letting Louise know how little of a rival she was. But that, while she kept her pact with Cabot, was a pay-off which was denied to her.

Their time in Tangier had been a continual round of business lunches and dinners, and Louise persuaded Cabot to a final party for the eve of their sailing from Tangier, dismissing his demur that on their last full day he and Felipe had business over in Gibraltar, with an airy, 'No problem, surely? Danielle positively thrives on organising parties—don't you, darling?—so can't you leave it to her and Chef to come up with something super for our last night?'

Cabot said, 'I could—if I saw any reason for asking her to work on *her* last day. But no, if you want a party, we'll hold it somewhere else—say at the Riad. You know enough people now to invite, and Danielle can take a rest.' He turned to Danielle. 'Care for a flip to Gib, sweetheart? Felipe and I will be working, but you could do the tourist thing and feed the apes, and we'd meet you for lunch at the Rock, and we should be back, if we clinch our deal, in time to dress for the evening.'

But Danielle, who had done 'the tourist thing' in Gibraltar, preferred a day at leisure where she was. She would swim, have coffee and watch the morning promenade from the patio of the Café de Paris, go for a light lunch at Forte's and take a siesta in the afternoon. 'Take Gina over to Gib with you,' she suggested. 'You could hand her over to one of the tourist parties climbing the Rock, and the apes would be just her scene'—an idea with which Gina fell in, claiming she had 'just about had the Arabian Nights thing in Tangier' and wouldn't mind something a bit more British for a change.

On the morning of the party there were flowers

for Danielle from Cabot—a corsage spray of white-petalled orchids tipped with green nestling in a perspex box.

When she thanked him he flipped a credit card across the table to her. 'Match it with something new and glamorous tonight,' he said.

She shook her head. 'I don't need to buy anything.'

'Nonsense,' he dismissed. 'Don't pretend that when I pressganged you into this job, you didn't promise yourself you'd milk me for every out-of-reach luxury you craved!'

That was so near the truth of her resolve to equip herself as if for the star role in a stage play—so artificial she had felt her part to be—that she visibly flushed, and Cabot laughed. Why had he to be so shrewd?

'I thought as much,' he nodded. 'So go ahead and surprise me tonight.' He tilted his head and appraised her shamelessly. 'To go with the orchids, something white and—virginal perhaps, suggesting to our friends that we're keeping to the rules and our first time has yet to come?' he offered coolly.

Not trusting herself to take him up on the cynical mockery of that, she said, 'Very well. I'll see what I can do,' and sweeping up the unopened florist's box, took it to the galley for it to be put on ice.

He should have his virginal dress if she had to scour every quarter of the city for it, she resolved. But she hadn't to go any farther than the most exclusive salon on the Boulevard Pasteur, where there was pearly organza waiting to float and sink in soft folds from her waist; the gown's one shoulder bare, the other shoulder and arm draped and sleeved to the wrist, a contrast in sophistication and modesty that pleased her and for which she proffered Cabot's credit card, deliberately refraining from asking its cost before she chose it.

She bought evening sandals the green of the orchid's petal-tips, had her hair set and a manicure, by which time it was too late for her swim, and remembering that Simon would be alone, she went back to the yacht.

She found him in Cabot's study, surrounded by papers, and typing at speed. 'Shall we have lunch together?' she asked, but he shook his head.

'No time for lunch,' he said. He sat back and flexed his fingers. 'No time, if I'm to break the back of this lot and still get the light I want——'

'The light? Oh, you've got a painting you haven't finished?' Danielle questioned.

'And shan't now. It's of that corner of the Great Socco—by that bar, the Pêche d'or—you know?'

'Where the flower women sit outside?'

'Yes. But it'll be in shadow in the next hour or two and the flower sellers pack up mid-afternoon. And I've got all this that I promised the Chief I'd finish. So it's curtains for the sketch, you see. I can't finish here *and* get to the medina in time.'

Danielle frowned, 'What a pity. It's your last chance for the noon hours; we shan't be here to-morrow. But couldn't you go over to the Great Socco now to catch the light and get down to this again when you get back?'

Simon riffled through the pile of papers beside the typewriter. 'Doubtful if I could do it before the Chief gets back and we go out this evening.'

'What is it, anyway? Just copy typing?'

'Yes—a report. Straightforward enough, but just bulk.'

'Well,' Danielle offered, 'I can type well enough to cope with that. So you cut along and do your stuff with the sketch, and maybe there won't be so much for you to finish before we go out. But don't be too late to do that and to change. We're leaving for the Riad at seven.'

Simon hardly waited to thank her before he was off, promising he would be back in good time. Knowing Louise was spending the day in the city with some new acquaintances, Danielle lunched alone and set about her task in the afternoon. She was able to get it to the point where Simon would have only to check and correct the pile of manuscript, but he had not returned by the time she went on deck to find that a most unusual fog had cut visibility to a few yards and was thick over the Straits. She was peering into it in dismay as Louise came aboard. 'Did you send for this from England?' Louise grumbled, and Danielle said, 'I'm wondering about the men's flight back from Gib,' when the telephone rang in Cabot's office.

'Danielle? There's this awful murk,' said Cabot on the line. 'The Tangier flight won't take off and the evening ferry has already crept out. So we're pinioned here until the fog lifts, which the wise-acres here say it may in a couple of hours.'

'It's thick here too, and that means you'll be late for going to the Riad?' said Danielle. 'Shall I cancel?'

'Oh no. If that weather reading is right, we shouldn't be too late getting in, but you and Simon and Louise had better go on, and we'll join you there as soon as we can.'

'But you'll ring again if you have to stay the night?'

'Of course, but that's not likely, we're told. By the way, Gina's lost that Union Jack headscarf she was sporting in honour of Gib. One of the Rock apes took a fancy to it and ate it.'

Danielle laughed, 'So much for patriotism!' and rang off. These were the kind of terms in which she was comfortable with Cabot. Sometimes she wondered how she would have reacted to him if she were his genuine employee, if he hadn't asked this masquerade of their engagement from her. She would have been happier. But would she have been so challenged, so intensely aware of the man's every look or word or touch? Would he have been so *important* to her?

The fog was beginning to thin by the time they planned to leave for the hotel. But by then Simon had not reappeared, though it was almost dusk and he could not possibly have been painting until then. Danielle had at last to give in to Louise's impatience to be on their way, and left a note with the deck steward to be given to Simon as soon as he turned up.

The Riad, on the one-time site of the Sultan's gardens, was unique among Tangier hotels. In architecture, decor, cuisine, it was wholly Eastern in character. The tessellated floors were carpeted in Persian rugs, the doors and partitions were of ornate ironwork, the arches of the traditional horseshoe design, the staff all in the fez and the enveloping brown cloth djellabah and the silent-

soled babouches of the upturned toe. The lighting,
by lantern and candle, owed nothing to electricity,
and a fair amount of the cooking was done over
braziers and on spits in full view of the patrons.

As soon as she and Louise arrived Danielle asked
the maître d'hotel to hold back dinner for their
party, and then they apologised to his guests for
Cabot's delay. In this Danielle had the impression
that, as long as the fun was on, the lateness of the
host was neither here nor there. People had come
to enjoy themselves and were already doing just
that.

She, however, was on edge, though more for
Simon to turn up than for the others, who must
surely be on their way since the fog had cleared.
But it was they, over an hour later, who arrived
first, having come on to the hotel after going back
to *Pandora* to change. Danielle was dancing when
Cabot came to find her, signalling to her to excuse
herself to her partner, while he stood by with a
face like thunder.

She went to him.

'What does this mean?' he demanded.

She looked at the paper he was thrusting at her.
'It's a message I left for Simon for when he got back.'

'Telling him you and Louise were leaving—I've
read it. But "got back"—from where? He had no
business to be anywhere but on board all day. He
had two or three hours' work to finish and check.
The typing is finished, but it hasn't been checked.
So where was he—and still is, apparently—that it
wasn't done?'

'You mean—he still hadn't come when you——?'
Danielle faltered.

'If he had, wouldn't Rahman have given him your note?'

'I suppose so. Rahman should have done.'

'He hadn't the chance. Simon hasn't shown up since Rahman saw him go ashore in the early afternoon. Well?'

Danielle explained. 'Simon needed the light to complete a watercolour he was doing in the medina. He'd have no other chance after today, so I told him to go, and I finished the typing for him.'

She met the hard glitter of Cabot's eyes. 'You took it upon yourself to take over confidential work he was supposed to be doing for me?' Cabot pressed.

'He didn't say it was confidential, and the text of it was only so much business reporting to me. Anyway, I did give him permission to go, and I apologise. But does that matter so much against the fact that he hasn't come back yet, when he could have done hours ago?'

Cabot growled. 'Of course not. I'm glad you appreciate the priorities. Where was he supposed to be going?' She told him. 'Six or seven hours ago, and three of them dark,' he calculated under his breath, crushed her note in his fist and turned away.

She came up again to his side. He couldn't leave her just like that! 'What are you going to do?' she asked.

'What do you think? If he hasn't gone back to *Pandora* by now—go in search of him, of course.' Cabot strode on, but she caught up with him, snatched at his sleeve.

'I know just where——' she pleaded. 'Take me with you, please.'

He shook free of her hold. 'Stay where you are,' he ordered. 'You may have done more harm than you know.'

CHAPTER SIX

FOR some minutes she had stared after him, dumb-founded by his accusation. Then she had run, out under the lanterns of the main entrance and, breathless and dishevelled by the night wind which had driven away the fog, had come level with him again as he opened the door of his parked car.

He turned on her. 'I thought I told you——?'

'You told me nothing I've a right to know, if Simon has come to any harm through me,' she retorted.

'None of which I'm going to stop to explain.'

'You don't have to. I'm coming with you. Open the passenger door, please, and let me in.'

If opposing wills were audible they might have been heard clashing. Then Cabot leaned from his own seat, unlocked her door, and she got in beside him.

'What use you imagine you can be, I've no idea. You hadn't even the sense to bring your wrap. And those things——' the toe of his shoe indicated the green sandals—'Have you no conception of what the lanes of the medina are like at night?' Cabot scorned.

'I can guess. But there was no time to go to the cloakroom, and I had to catch you. As for being of use, how can you expect anything of me, if I don't know what danger you're afraid of for

Simon? He often goes to the medina alone to paint or sketch.'

'And stays for seven hours, during half of which he couldn't see to work, and when he's known there was a deadline for his getting back? Likely this time, would you say?'

'But what could——?' Danielle began. But they were on the quay now, alongside Pandora's berth, and Cabot was out of the car and going aboard. When he came back he shook his head. 'No joy,' he said. 'The Great Socco now, and that bar.' But he did not drive off at once. 'You wouldn't know that Simon has had a drug problem?' he asked.

Danielle said, 'I did know. He was quite frank about it soon after you brought him on the trip. But he didn't want Gina told.'

'Yes, well, he'd kicked it successfully in England. But in a city with the reputation of this one—where drug-taking is a habit, not a crime—there's as much temptation on every street corner as there is to an alcoholic in the nearest bar.'

'But if Simon was cured, surely he wouldn't fall again?'

Cabot shrugged. 'You'd hope not. I'd trust not. But if he did, his instinct would be to escape the consequences by staying away. Or he could be in no fit state *to* come back. In either case, where is he in this maze? But he has to be found—tonight, and by me, if we're to sail tomorrow without the newshounds licking their chops over "English Tycoon's Yacht Held up in Port. Owner's Drug-Addict Secretary Missing. According to a Spokesman——" and all the rest of the blah. Now do you understand?'

Danielle was half tempted to question whether he was concerned the more for Simon or for the scandal. But she said, 'yes, though I could hardly have foreseen the risk when I let him go this afternoon, could I?'

'You'd have done better not to override my orders to him,' Cabot said curtly, and then, 'But that's water under the bridge now. Let's find this bar.'

He drove up through the nearest ancient gateway to the old town where, by contrast with the night life of the European quarter, the frenzy of the daytime activity in the market squares had given place to shadowed dimness and silence. It would begin all over again at dawn with the influx of the country traders bringing in their wares for sale, but tonight only a few figures moved and disappeared in the darkness.

'This the place?' Cabot had stopped outside a cladded wooden building painted in dark maroon as background to a design of golden fish under the name sign *La Pêche d'Or*. Light showed round the closed door and through chinks in the cladding, and there was noise and raucous music inside.

Danielle said, 'Yes. Simon says it's French-owned, not Moroccan, so it sells alcohol to the French and Spanish and to tourists. He's had a drink there and a snack once or twice when he's been sketching outside.'

'So they may remember him, or may have seen him leave. Wait here in the car, and I'll go in. Lock your door,' Cabot ordered.

Ten minutes later he came back. 'Nothing doing,' he reported. 'I drank a couple of *pastis* in quick order with an eye to easing relations, but they see me as Authority with a capital A, and they're as dumb and glassy-eyed as their painted fish. No one knows Simon; no one ever saw him sketching; if he ever bought a drink he was one of too many customers to remember. And yet——' Cabot paused and pulled at his bottom lip in thought—'I could swear they do know something, and they aren't getting involved.'

'You think there's something they could tell you if they would?' Danielle asked.

'I'm pretty sure of it. They're so over-tense.'

'Well, suppose——? No, let me think for a moment,' she checked his question, then asked, 'Is there a woman there, or some men?'

'Only a middle-aged one, serving, whom I take to be the Madame of the house.'

'Well, could I perhaps soften the authority idea by appealing to her as one woman to another? You are—only my fiancé, and Simon is—yes, my brother, I think, and he's young and wild and I'm desperate for news of him. So if she could give me the smallest clue—Do you think it might work?' Danielle appealed.

Cabot allowed, 'It well could, if you put it over with that look and in that tone. Melting, both of them. Do you want to try?'

'Please. Were you speaking English?'

'No, I managed in French, and I imagine you can.'

Against the stridency of the amplified accordion music there was a stir and then a hush when they entered the bar, and Cabot ushered Danielle to a table, himself going to the counter and waiting to get Madame's attention.

Someone gave a wolf whistle in Danielle's direction. She smiled acknowledgement of it; encouraged, one or two other men made noises appreciative of her looks and the white dress, and she felt she had been accepted.

After some earnest talk with Madame at the bar, Cabot brought her over. A boy followed with drinks for the three of them, and when she and Madame had shaken hands and she had admired the bar's décor, Danielle ventured on her act of appeal to Madame's sympathies, though it was Cabot who broke the ice with, 'My fiancée's brother, you understand, madame? She is distraught.'

'Yes, yes.' Madame drank her absinthe in short, nervous sips, but added nothing more. Danielle leaned forward to take her hand in her own. 'He is young, madame. He speaks only his own language, and he does not know the city well. Naturally I am very troubled for him. He is fair, with a short beard—so——' Danielle demonstrated—'and his manner is quiet. Are you *quite* sure, madame, that neither you nor any of your patrons have seen him today or at any other time?'

Madame sipped again, then found her tongue. 'There is trouble for him if he is found?' she asked.

'Trouble? Why, no!'

'Nor for any of those who might know something about the boy? Monsieur here is not of the police?'

'*No*! He is just my fiancé and as anxious as I am. So you could help us, madame, if you would?'

'H'm. I must speak to my man.' Madame left

the table and went back to the bar. After whispering to her husband she signalled from there, 'Come,' and when Danielle and Cabot joined her, she said with now no show of reluctance, 'The boy is here, in our home—upstairs. Come.'

'Here?' They followed her out of the bar, along a dark stone passage, through a wine-celler lined with casks and up a staircase to a landing where Madame opened a door to a room in which, under a coverlet, Simon lay on the bed, deeply asleep. He did not wake nor stir when Madame put a match to the wick of a lamp and turned it up.

Danielle uttered a long 'Oh-h!' and Cabot went to feel Simon's pulse. 'He has been so for how long?' he asked the woman.

She shrugged. 'Four—five hours. Since they left him and went off.'

'Since *who* left him?'

'Des butors.' She used the word for 'louts'. Three, four of them.'

'Moroccans?'

'No—your kind. English, American, I do not know. They were seen watching him paint and laughing with him. Then they all come into our bar and order, and laugh more and make tumult, and when the others go, they leave this one as nearly insensible as now.'

'They were all right themselves?'

'They could walk. He could not. No doubt they make play of putting something evil in his wine. But it is nothing they get from us.'

Cabot soothed, 'One didn't suppose so, madame.'

'Nevertheless, one cannot always convince the

police. And so we think it best to take the unfortunate into our home until he wakes up, when he may tell who his friends were. For they should be punished.'

'I doubt if he knew them, or whether you will ever see them again,' said Cabot. 'Meanwhile, my fiancée is most grateful to you, madame. But in thanking you for your kindness, may we ask one more favour of you? A pot of strong black coffee for the young man, to help him to wake enough for us to put him in our car and take him home?'

'But of course, monsieur. But do not hurry him. I shall send up a cognac too.'

'Send three,' he invited. 'And, madame——' As Danielle went to sit by Simon, he edged the woman into a corner where, after a short gesticulatory argument, a bunch of paper money went from his wallet to the pocket of her apron, and she departed, smiling. A minute or two later before the coffee arrived, Simon stirred and opened his eyes.

An hour later he had recovered sufficiently for Suli, the night steward, to be given charge of him and to see him into bed. When he had come to, his memory of his ordeal was hazy, but his story had borne out Madame's as far as it went. He had been about to pack up his gear mid-afternoon when these four young tourists of about his own age had struck up an acquaintance and they had all gone for a drink. But from the second filling of his glass he remembered nothing more until he had waked to find Danielle at his strange bedside. What had happened to him in between?

'You were drugged,' Cabot had told him. To

which Simon had reacted violently.

'I was *not*! I've neither seen nor touched a grain of the stuff since———!'

Cabot repeated, '*Were* drugged—passive tense. Keep your cool. Those bright sparks who picked you up must have slipped you some kind of narcotic for fun.'

'Oh.' Simon had considered this. 'But you can't know they did, and you could believe I———'

Cabot had cut him short. 'I could, but I don't. If you'd doped yourself, you'd have done it to get some fun out of a high. You wouldn't have settled for slumping into five hours or so of dead sleep. So get to your own bed now, and count yourself lucky we shan't have to cancel tomorrow's sailing for you.'

For Danielle the evening could well have ended there. She was not so much physically tired as she felt mentally drained by the doubts and fears of the episode. But Cabot intended to return to the party and expected her to go with him.

'As host, I haven't exactly been in evidence yet,' he said. 'And you'll have been missed too.'

She smiled rather wearily. 'Probably only by Gina, who'll be wondering why Simon isn't there.'

'Which, thanks be, can easily be explained with the truth that he was taken for a ride by those corner boys. No fault of his but gullibility.'

'You were afraid, like me, that it could have been his own doing, and that we'd have to lie to keep his secret?' she questioned.

'Afraid? The understatement of the year! I'd begun to be scared yellow that he'd ratted on me,

showing I'd failed with him, which is something
I shouldn't care to take.'

Danielle said quietly, 'I can imagine. You hate
failing in anything, don't you?'

'Who doesn't?' he countered dismissingly. It was
only a grudge of an admission that he knew he had
an Achilles heel, but it took her one step nearer to
her original goal of learning the make-up of the
enemy she had taken on. From there she found
herself thinking that it would be easier to regard
him as an enemy if he acted like one all the time
and not, as tonight, like a caring, concerned friend
who valued her help in a difficult situation.

They had been missed by their guests, people
claiming to suspect they had escaped to some private haunt for a romantic purpose about which
there were some coy jokes and arch comments.
Only their own party questioned Simon's absence,
and to them they explained briefly what had
happened to him. Danielle felt that it hardly regis-
tered with Louise or Felipe, both far into the festive
scene, and Gina's reaction was a tart, 'You'd think he
was big enough, old enough and ugly enough to
know about refusing sweets from strangers,' followed
by an undisguisedly anxious, 'He *is* all right?'

The dancing, the talk and the drinking went on
very late, to a point of near-exhaustion for
Danielle, nerve-strained by Simon's affair and her
role as co-hostess to Cabot. She was only too
thankful when with a few practised, urbane hints
he indicated that, regretfully, the evening was at an
end and their guests began to take their leave.

He, Danielle, Felipe and Gina met in the foyer.
Louise did not appear. 'She said she was going on

somewhere with some people, and that they would be seeing her back to *Pandora*,' Felipe told Cabot.

'Where were they going on?' Cabot asked.

But Felipe either hadn't heard or couldn't remember which night-club they had had in mind. 'Just on somewhere; he repeated foolishly, and with an impatient 'Huh!' Cabot went to bring up his car.

Arrived on board, Gina went to bed after Danielle had ruled that she couldn't look in on Simon. Danielle said goodnight to the men and went herself, leaving Felipe persuading Cabot that without one more drink as a nightcap, he was sure he couldn't sleep.

In her cabin Danielle sank into a chair, feeling almost too weary to undress. She sat for a long time, head drooped, hands emptily relaxed in her lap, until she realised she was beginning to nod, and that the process of undressing had to be faced.

The night was hot; she soon thrust off the single sheet she usually needed and soon after that she knew she was drowsing deliciously into sleep, though for how long she couldn't tell when she woke with a start to find herself covered again and the sheet drawn taut across her body by the weight of something—someone?—resting upon it.

She struggled up, knuckling her eyes. A hand— *Cabot's hand*—on her shoulder pushed her down again.

She stared at him. He wore no pyjama top under his short dressing-robe, she noticed. 'What are you doing here? How did you get in? How long——?' she demanded.

His mouth lifted in a half-smile. 'I took advantage of our shared bathroom—you hadn't locked that door. And how long have I been watching you sleep? Not too long. Not too irksomely long at all,' he said.

'But what do you want?'

'Originally to ask you to bear with me until Louise chooses to return.'

'Must you wait up for her?'

'Not necessarily, though Suli willl let me know when she arrives, and waiting for her seemed a good excuse for calling on you,' he confessed blandly.

'Calling on me? Intruding would be a better word. Do you realise what time it must be?' Danielle retorted, her heart quickening. What did he really want?

'You can tell me—you're wearing your watch. But at a guess I'd say it's the ideal time for the privacy we so seldom get. Tonight—for my chance to congratulate you on the success you made of the evening; Tangier circles should be quoting it as a party for years. And tonight again—to thank you for the credit you did me with everyone who saw you looking as radiant as you did. And if by chance you had anything appreciative to say to me, don't you agree it would be a pity to keep any of it on ice until the morning?'

She didn't know what to reply. This tolerant raillery, verging almost on flirtation, was another facet of the man; engaging enough in its appeal to make her reluctant to snub him for assuming he could walk in on her at this hour and find himself welcomed. She said, though not sharply, '*My* need of privacy doesn't seem to have occurred to you.

Nor my right to regard my cabin as my own.'

'Oh, but it did!' His eyes had widened ingenuously. He *was* flirting with her! He stood and
pulled back the sheet he must have drawn over
her. 'As soon as I saw you were carelessly asleep
with nothing but that revealing nightgown to cover
you, it was obvious you were counting on enough
privacy to protect you from unexpected callers. So,
being one myself, and hoping to be allowed to stay,
I decided to spare your blushing modesty when you
woke, and tucked you in. No, don't take it back.
It's served its turn——' This last was in reply to
her grab for the sheet, which he stripped down to
the bottom of the bed and left there.

'When you found I was asleep you'd have been
better advised to leave me to it and go back the
way you came,' she muttered.

'Wasting a time and a place that took all my
audacity to contrive?'

'You had to make use of some luck too,' she
pointed out.

'In finding you get-at-able without having to
keep my foot in the door? That too,' Cabot agreed.
'My star was in the ascendant.' Hands in the
pockets of his robe, he stood looking down at her.
'But now I'm here, and you are, mightn't we try
putting some more zing into our relationship?
You'll remember I told you we had a right to get
some enjoyment out of its necessity? But how much
practice in enjoying each other have we had since
then? None at all!'

'A lot of other things have happened between us
since then.'

'Ardour-cooling things? A few—minor clashes,

silly resentments, empty threats—But none of them serious enough, surely, to cheat an ordinarily virile man of making the most of his workaday partnership with an extraordinarily attractive woman ... *Surely?*'

She had known his intention all along; known that in keeping him talking on his chosen facetious level, she had been playing for time—time to quell the unbidden surge of excitement he roused in her, as much as time in which to call all the forces of her will to resist him.

But now time had run out. With the question he hadn't waited for her to answer, he had gathered her up to him, lain her none too gently back on the bed, himself beside her, above her, his hands tangling in her hair, cupping her face, making nothing of the ribbon ties on her shoulders, baring them in turn to his kiss.

At his lips' touch it was as if an electric current ran thrillingly through her, body and nerves betraying her will in a sensuous craving to respond, to give, to experience, to use and be sweetly used by a mutual desire which, while it lasted, could be blindly oblivious of the hard facts of an enmity which, in the cold sanity of everyday, seemed so compelling. Here and now pure sensation was taking over from reason, and if she yielded to her delight in the searching demands of his mouth and hands as she longed to, that would be primitive woman and man seeking pleasure in each other— and the temptation to surrender was very great.

Later she might be ashamed, self-hating. But that would be Danielle Kane, balanced and controlled again. Nothing to do with the avid, sentient crea-

ture for whom this scene, without past or future to
justify it, was the only reality she wanted. She put
up both her hands to Cabot's mane of auburn
hair, drew his head down and cradled it on her
breast, signalling her abandonment to the madness
that had her in its grip. For a long moment he was
still, then his murmured 'Ah-h' acknowledged his
conquest. Thigh to thigh with her, body to body,
his arms crushed the breath from her lungs and the
pressure of his mouth stifled the little whimpers of
desire that parted her lips. He was emboldened,
daring her to deny him the ultimate in submission
to the satiation of a physical hunger which, from
him to her, could not be love, but merely . . . car-
nality. Pure lust, no more—but was her own
hunger for his body any different? Was she only
lusting too?

At the question the dark tide of sensation
receded, leaving her tossed and bruised on the arid
shore of reason. She was no voluptuary, recklessly
thirsting to be gratified. She was Danielle Kane,
with dignity and pride to guard, and the death of
an injured woman to remember against this man
at her side.

She tore herself free from his grasp. She panted,
'No——' and again 'No'—— ' the last denial in-
audible against the noise of a scuffling agitation
from the corridor outside.

'What the——?' Cabot swung down from the
bed. Danielle remembered he had expected Suli to
tell him when Louise returned, but before she could
warn him not to open to Suli from her cabin, he
was at the door, confronting Felipe on the threshold.

Felipe, slightly sobered though not wholly, was leaning on the door jamb. 'It's Louise,' he said thickly. 'She is back, and Suli came to tell you. But you weren't in your cabin, and now she won't come aboard unless you come and fetch her. She's as tight as a——'

Cabot was tying the sash of his robe. 'Who brought her back?' he asked.

'Zuleikerman Hedjaz—the Kedhour cork estate man.'

'Did he dump her on the quay and leave her?'

'No. She is still in his car and he wants to get——' With that, the door closed on Cabot, who had stepped out into the corridor, and Danielle, left shivering, as if with the aftermath of shock, heard no more.

She slid off the bed, looking back at it with distaste. How much had Felipe seen of her, or taken in? Not that it mattered, she supposed. It was enough that Felipe knew Suli hadn't found Cabot in the master cabin but that he had appeared from hers. Fuddled as he still was, Felipe could make much of that—the very last thing of which she wanted to be suspected, that she was anticipating her fictitious marriage to Cabot, even though Louise's sly mind may already have concluded it was so.

But it was too late now. Felipe would pass on what he had seen, and from now until the end of the cruise she would have to live with the smear that there was little difference between her behaviour and the brand of easy virtue which had taken Louise to Cabot's cabin uninvited on a certain other night. Perhaps on even more than one.

The one sop to Danielle's pride was that her self-command had brought her to her senses before Felipe's arrival. The 'No' which had been wrung from her had been her own will's protest at her dangerously near surrender. She must make Cabot understand this when he returned from dealing with Louise's vagaries.

His approach had only been an exercise in sexual power, and she had to convince him that though she had responded, it had been on much the same exploratory level, and she had always kept a tight rein on her ability to call a halt to action she hadn't invited and didn't welcome.

And she had done just that—withdrawn, dealt him the cut direct at the point where she had led him to believe that his dominance had her at her mercy . . .

That little of this was true did not keep her from rehearsing it as if it were. But though she waited and listened for him for a long time, Cabot had not come back to her before she slept. Where had he spent the rest of the night? With Louise?

He was not in his cabin when she went to breakfast, which she was to take alone. Cabot had earlier gone ashore on Customs business, taking Simon with him, the table steward told her, and he thought Gina was watching the cleaning and refilling of the pool. Neither Louise nor Felipe appeared—both of them enjoying hangovers, Danielle concluded maliciously. After breakfast she went to the galley to check the menu for an early lunch before *Pandora* sailed at two o'clock.

When she returned to the sundeck an hour later Louise was stretched on a lounger, sipping from a glass of iced lime water. She lifted a nonchalant hand to Danielle. 'How is our invalid this morning?' she asked.

'Simon? He must be quite recovered, I think. He's gone with Cabot to the Customs House,' said Danielle.

'Talk of innocents abroad! You'd think that at his age he could spot a gaggle of drug-pushers at fifty yards!'

'They weren't pushers, he said. Simply a bunch of young tourists who must have thought it fun to put him out by slipping some dope into his drink.'

'Did they rob him?'

'No. Just left him asleep in the bar; even left his sketching block and his paints beside him,' said Danielle.

'The idiocies the young find amusing these days!' Louise mourned limply, dismissing the subject and closing her eyes with a sigh. After a minute or two she murmured, 'Lovely party last night. And even more exciting, the aftermath. Seiyid Hedjaz has the most fabulous villa out at Kedhour, and there were just he and I, alone.'

'I thought you went to a night-club with a party?' Danielle questioned.

'We did, but we dropped them later, after the floor show. You and Cabot should have come on with us. The night was still young.'

'Too old by then to prop me up, I'm afraid. I was dead tired and went straight to bed.'

'But not straight to sleep, did you?' Louise hinted.

'*Straight* to sleep, after I'd gathered enough will to undress,' Danielle insisted. Battle was joined, she knew, but she would lose it with as much dignity as she could.

'No doubt to refresh yourself for the tryst you were keeping with Cabot much later?'

'When Felipe had to fetch him to you and found him in my cabin?' Danielle asked cruelly. 'That was no tryst. He'd seen that my light was still on and came to see if I were still awake.'

'Ah. Well, that wasn't *quite* the impression Felipe got, from the tale he told me this morning. Cabot couldn't have been just *passing* your cabin, because he was undressed too.'

'Though I should doubt whether Felipe was in any fit state to get a clear impression of anything he saw from the corridor,' Danielle retorted.

'Well, of course one knows he does get rather under the weather,' Louise conceded. 'He could have been wrong. But there, dear——' she patted Danielle's hand patronisingly—'why deny *to me* that you and Cabot were enjoying a roll in the hay? You're engaged to the man, aren't you, and it's being done all the time nowadays. Perhaps, if you've been keeping him at arm's length, you should be thankful it was with you and not with some little pick-up from the party. Men do expect their oats——' she finished coarsely.

'Which Cabot wasn't getting and won't get from me,' Danielle managed, as she snatched back and her hand turned away. Last word she might have had, but from the conspiratorial little chuckle behind her, she knew she hadn't convinced Louise.

CHAPTER SEVEN

Pandora left punctually to time that afternoon, her next port of call Alicante on the Spanish coast, a matter of two days' sail. At lunch Louise had claimed surprise and annoyance that Cabot planned no days of leisure ashore either there or at Barcelona.

'I thought we should be stopping off at all sorts of exciting places. Nor anywhere chic on the Riviera?' she questioned.

'Not until Monte Carlo,' Cabot told her. 'I've no business to do in Spain, and Felipe and I have a conference date to keep in Monaco.'

'I should have been warned. I have friends spending the summer in St Tropez—English people among them, and I told them we should almost certainly drop in on our way. Can't we?'

'You can have an hour or two ashore wherever we refuel or need stores. But Carlos could have told you this was primarily a business trip, not a millionaire's dawdle round the Mediterranean.'

'I thought it was a kind of pre-marriage honeymoon for you and Danielle! But do you mean there's no way I can see these people in St Tropez?'

'We can drop you off there, if you like.'

'And Felipe?'

'No, I need Felipe.'

'And how should I meet up with you in Monte Carlo?'

'By road or air, I suppose.'

She nodded. 'I might do that. I'll think about it,' she agreed, and had flashed a smile at Danielle across the table, addressing her, but talking *at* Cabot. 'No hope, I'm afraid, darling, that Milord would let you have a few days off duty ashore with me. I might lead you into who knows what kind of temptation in a place like St Tropez!'

To which Cabot had returned a cool, 'And how right you are at that. No hope whatsoever. Danielle stays on board.'

Alone with Danielle later, Gina spoke for both of them when she quoted, ' "For this relief, much thanks,"—that's one of the few bits of Shakespeare I know, by the way. Because you do agree, don't you, that Louise is the *end* for general unlikeableness all round?' she pressed Danielle.

Danielle said guardedly, 'I admit she's not one of my favourite people, but——'

'But nothing!' Gina exploded. 'I tell you, ever, *ever* so delicately the woman trails poison wherever she goes. D'you know, this morning she tried to put me off Simon—poor innocent Simon—by saying we didn't *have* to believe his story of being doped by strangers. How could we tell he hadn't gone off on a drug jape himself? So I said of course we all knew he spent every penny of his salary on drugs and went on a trip every night, and it was a scream, watching her wondering whether to believe me, before it dawned that the joke was on her. She wasn't exactly amused, I'm afraid. But she shouldn't be so gullible. Imagine—young, earnest-as-they-come Simon a drug fiend! I mean, there's a laugh!' Gina concluded, unaware of how little a 'laugh' must have been the battle which Simon had earlier fought and won.

'I haven't told you about my day in Gib,' she went on. 'I got off with a young man! We were both feeding bananas to the apes on the Rock, and he'd have tried to rescue the headscarf one of them snatched, if I hadn't told him I didn't want it back halfchewed. So then we talked and exchanged names. His was Hunter, and he said he was just idling round the Mediterranean coast; he might get as far as Italy. I told him about us, who I was, and about Cabot and you, and though of course he'd never heard of me, he knew quite a bit about Cabot; since he'd escaped with you on this cruise, back in London anything about you both was news, and as a journalist, he—Colin Hunter— would appreciate whatever I could tell him about you that he might use as a scoop.'

Danielle caught her breath. 'That was pretty slick. What paper does he write for?'

'None specially. He's freelance, and a scoop would be something nobody else got hold of, and that he would give to only one paper if he got it. That way he'd make money and maybe have a chance of getting on the staff. So what about it? Could I help?'

'He sounds like a real go-getter. What did you say?' Danielle asked.

'I snubbed him. He was snooping too much. I told him there was nothing I knew that he didn't seem to know already. But he was unsquashable. He asked where we were finishing up, and when I

said Monte Carlo, he insisted on my taking a tele-
phone number where he could be reached there.
He wanted me to go and have an ice or coffee in
the town, but I was meeting Cabot and Felipe and
I tore up the note of his number and threw it away.
End of Romantic Encounter on the Rock.'

Danielle laughed with relief at the young man's
rout. But the incident worried her, lest she and
Cabot were of enough interest for some enterpris-
ing newshounds to follow them up and ask questions, too many of the questions about the background to their supposed engagement which Cabot
had bid to escape by leaving on the cruise. She
looked into the unknown future ahead, to the day
which Cabot had refused to specify, the day when
he had no further use for her services and they
would concoct a plausible reason for their parting,
their romance a fallen meteor, and herself no longer
a part of the Cabot Steele notoriety.

On that day, if the world let Cabot keep his
secret until then, she would be free of the
overweight masquerade he had contrived for his
self-interested purposes; she would be no longer
committed to a lie, but her own woman again, her
private score with Cabot brought out into the open
and settled by his learning that he could never have
persuaded her to his will if she hadn't had some
self-interested purpose too.

That showdown had to come before they parted
for good, and she mustn't lose her zest for it along
the way . . .

She could have wished she wasn't present when
Gina repeated her story to the others at
dinner, but if she expected Cabot to show the con-

cern she had felt, she was mistaken.

'You shouldn't have sent the poor lad away hungry; you should have made up something to tell him,' Felipe advised.

'Like what?'

'Well, some date for their marriage, or some details of Danielle's trousseau, for instance. He could make quite a few bylines out of that.'

Louise drawled, 'He could make a good many more if Gina had hinted that Cabot had some dark reason of his own for running away from the publicity.'

Gina turned hostile eyes Louise-ward. 'I ought to have thought of that. Like showing the media he wasn't having it come between him and Danielle as it has done before? I mean, we've all heard about——'

She was cut short in mid-sentence by Cabot, his tone splintering with ice, yet fully controlled as he said, 'Dark reasons and secrets I promise you in plenty if you care to keep your date with the young pup in Monte Carlo, hm?'

'I can't. I don't want to. I told you, I tore up his phone number,' Gina muttered, evidently reading the rebuke.

'What a pity. Because, between now and then, Danielle and I could have fun compiling a whole catalogue of my reasons for carrying her off. But no? You're not interested? Good. And neither are we in the random probings of the press—are we?' Cabot turned for confirmation to Louise, whose delicate sniff signified her bored indifference to the subject.

Simon had returned from his morning errands ashore with a sheaf of flowers for Danielle——' a little thank-you for coping with my stupidity,' he had explained sheepishly. But she was not alone with Cabot all day, and when she and Louise and Gina went to their cabins at the end of the evening, they left the men in the saloon.

She did not get ready for bed at once. Not by an eyelid's flicker during the day had Cabot admitted a memory of her rejection of him last night. But her resolve was still firm. If he came to her cabin before going to his own, then he must be left in no doubt that her 'No' to him had meant what it said; that she wasn't falling victim to his careless seduction again.

He came, as she thought he might. After his knock he waited for her to open to him, and then came no further than the threshold.

'I imagine I have to be freshly invited after my *gaffe* of last night?' he said.

She didn't understand him, '*gaffe*' being hardly the word for his practised temptation of her. Then light dawned. He *was* thinking only of his blunder in answering Felipe from her room; he had taken no account of her recoil seconds before; she was going to have to spell it out to him after all.

She said, 'You weren't invited last night. You came, you said, for one thing—to put in time, waiting for Louise. You stayed for quite another, again at no invitation from me.'

His brows went up. 'Not even implied?' He looked her over, appearing to sum up the rigidity of her figure, her withdrawn expression. 'All right. I realise there's no present welcome for me, and no wonder, considering how I brought the good news to Felipe, but last night wasn't there a certain—

willingness, an accepting, even in the end, desire? I wasn't mistaken in that? We were enjoying each other until Felipe——?'

'*Not* until Felipe!' she flared at him. 'I'd told you No already before that. Felipe didn't interrupt anything particularly exciting where I was concerned. I'm sorry if he did for you, but you're mistaken if you think I wanted any part in it, whatever it was.'

'Didn't you know what it was?'

'Yes! You were chancing your arm and hoping I'd fall for it.'

'And hadn't you fallen for it? If not, you put on a very realistic imitation.'

That was where she wanted him—in doubt of her surrender. 'As long as you realise I wasn't committed at all,' she insinuated.

'You want me to believe you were putting on an act?'

'It fooled you? I'm glad.'

There was a beat of silence before Cabot spoke. Then he said, 'You shouldn't be. It's a dangerous game that only cheats play. Common too—men have a word for women who make a practice of it. I rather thought you'd be above it, but if not——'

Danielle had expected to feel triumph, but she did not. He had been deceived by her ruse, but he despised her for it, and that stung. She retorted. 'Perhaps it was you who taught me to play-act in a difficult situation, and I learned my lesson too well to suit you.'

He shook his head. 'No. If last night was a performance, you've had an instinct for it from your cradle, and it was altogether too well rehearsed. It persuaded me I was giving as much pleasure as I was getting, and you can't do much worse harm to a man's ego than to take him just so far and then claim it was all a nonsense you didn't mean.'

'Pleasure!' she scorned. 'At my expense! If that's all you were after!'

'For the moment it was. For the few minutes I believed we were sharing it, yes. It seemed to me our reasonably smooth partnership entitled us to something more genuine than the scenes of bliss we lay on for our public, and I was robbing you of nothing you call expense while I thought I was inviting you to enjoyment.'

'Pleasure—full   stop?   Enjoyment—with   no strings!' she took him up. 'You claim you can turn them on like—like taps, and off again when you've had your fill?'

'Why not? In these days, isn't it known as heavy petting?' he countered cynically. 'Except that you'd have me believe that last night you never turned them on.'

Hadn't he really intended to make love to her to a point of no return, or was this his reprisal for the insult she had dealt his pride? She had to know. She said, 'But if I had—enjoyed you and had been willing——?' She stopped, shy of the question, and she got no answer to it.

With a shrug of indifference Cabot stepped back into the corridor. 'This is an extremely unrewarding post-mortem on things past,' he said. 'You won't be troubled in the same way again. But just a word of advice you won't take—don't practise that brand of twentieth-century coquetry too often, or some man in your future might make you very sorry.' The door shut, softly and finally behind him, leaving her defeated less by his skill in argument than by the despair of her failure to learn, from the various fronts he turned to her, who was the real Cabot Steele.

One facet she had reason to hate. Some perplexed her, some she found disarming—dangerously so for her mission. Others she could respect and find dependable; others again, his virility, his zest, his readiness for life, she could have loved in any other man than he. Perhaps in the one with whom Cabot's parting shot had threatened her? But he was only a shadowy figure on tomorrow's horizon. Cabot was today's problem—troubling, enigmatic, and very real.

She was always surprised and relieved by the ease of their relationship in public. The next day there was no sign of the overnight tensions between them. She took her cue from Cabot and acted to it to a point where she could almost believe that this was all there was; she was an engaged girl on a cruise with her attentive fiancé, not a spy, nor a minion, nor a pawn in someone else's game. When she fantasised this she was Danielle Kane, loving and loved, and her man was there beside her every day . . .

Pandora ploughed smoothly on, keeping to her schedule and making brief calls at Alicante and Barcelona, and a longer one at Marseilles. Louise went ashore at St Tropez, planning to rejoin the yacht in Monte Carlo in a few days' time. After passing within sight of Cannes and Nice journey's end was near, but Cabot was still noncommittal as to the length of his stay in Monte Carlo.

He brushed off Danielle's attempts to define it. He and Felipe had this week of conference first; he had Gina to deliver to her mother; he had other business to negotiate, architects and builders to consult; Felipe and Louise would want to sample the luxury Monaco had to offer. No, he couldn't name a date for *Pandora*'s departure. What was Danielle's hurry?

As if he couldn't guess! 'I have to make my own plans,' she told him. 'Aren't the Diegos flying to Paris and going back to Lisbon from there? And when you've settled Gina with Mrs Lisle, and aren't taking any other guests back to England, what further use can you have for me?'

'Refer back to the letter of our agreement,' he said crisply. 'It made no time limit to your assignment, and I could need your services for some time longer—while I'm here.'

'How so? And as what?'

'Continuing as my fiancée, of course. You'll be introduced so to any people we meet, and as we know Gina won't return her mother's welcome with any rapture on her side, you could help me with that. I can't dump her, gift-wrapped, on Mrs Lisle's doorstep, and expect there to be bliss and harmony between them from then on.'

'Do you expect there ever to be?' Danielle queried.

'I don't know, but a little time in the freedom of Monte Carlo might work wonders.'

'I shouldn't count on it.'

'Even if not, there's nothing Gina can do about it. Mrs Lisle is her legal guardian, and she is still a minor.'

'But still old enough to be married to a man of her mother's choice?'

Cabot said, 'We've only Beatrix Lisle's hints and Gina's sour speculations about that. The truth may be very different. Anyhow, I need your help in their teething period, which could last until my business is finished.' He paused to calculate. 'Let's see—we should dock in the yacht harbour in the early afternoon of Wednesday. Could you organise dinner on board for Beatrix that night?'

'I suppose so. I'll see about it. Will Gina be going ashore with her afterwards?'

'I don't know. I'll ring Beatrix as soon as we dock, and we shall have to play it by ear.' But as he turned away Danielle had another question to ask.

It was, 'And when you've finished in Monaco and Gina's settled, do you plan then to break our supposed engagement?'

He turned back to stare at her. 'After—what will it be?—probably six weeks in all? Of course not! We have to go back to England and, after a decent interval, end it there.'

'And what would you regard as a decent interval? I have my living to earn, and I must look for another job,' she reminded him.

His lip curled. 'Don't worry. When the time comes, I'll pay you redundancy money, but the timing may depend on as much or as little publicity as the newshounds will allow us. If we do it in the shadow of a major political crisis or a film star's eighth wedding, we could get away with it quietly. You must leave it to me.'

'*And* the reason for our breaking up, to you?'

'As I remember, I originally gave you a free

choice of that. You still have it,' he said coldly.

From the yacht basin modern Monte Carlo appeared as a conglomeration of skyscrapers vying with each other in height and geometric design and occupying every precious level square metre of rocky cliff. The property developers were even dropping more foundations into the foreshore, compensating with beaches of artificial shingle, and raising yet more scaffolding to support still more skeletal apartment blocks in the making. Just the place for Cabot Steele to meet with kindred souls, thought Danielle, though later she was to discover different cities—the one of nineteenth-century splendour and landscaped gardens, and another of narrow climbing streets and steps and ancient houses huddled round courtyards private to every intruder but the sun.

She and Gina left the yacht in the afternoon to walk up for tea at the Café de Paris and to stake out the forthcoming concert and ballet dates at the Casino. When they returned Gina flatly refused to change from slacks and workman's bib top for dinner with her mother.

'Why should I dress up?' she wanted to know. 'For me it's not exactly a gala occasion. More like the lamb to the slaughter, if I felt lamblike, which I don't.'

Nor, it seemed when Cabot brought her aboard in the evening, did Mrs Lisle regard the meeting with much pleasure.

She was a carefully groomed and coiffeured woman whose doll prettiness was marred by a downturned mouth, expressive of discontent and frustration. She greeted Gina with a conventional peck for each cheek, then held her off for a critical stare. She hooked a forefinger under the bib. 'Really, Gina—that garb! Is Cabot making you work your passage by swabbing the decks, or what?' she sneered.

Gina bridled. 'What's wrong with it? It's comfortable for anything I want to do.'

'For *evening*? For *my* first evening? And your *hair*!'

Gina's hand, thrusting through the offending hair, did nothing to improve its appearance, and Danielle ventured a peace-making, 'It's terribly difficult to keep one's hair tidy on deck,' which Mrs Lisle dismissed with a snort of disbelief.

Dinner was an uncomfortable meal, despite Cabot's expertise as a host, but Danielle was relieved that their guest's self-interest was such that she showed none of Louise's arch curiosity about Cabot's engagement. She accepted Danielle without question, uttered little noises of approval and congratulation to Cabot, was 'little woman' coy with Felipe and passed over Simon as if he were part of the furniture, before reverting to herself as the main subject of her conversation.

When they adjourned for coffee to the saloon, Gina lifted a beckoning thumb at Simon. 'Let's go find a disco. I've seen one along the front,' she said, and when Simon had looked at Cabot for permission, they departed.

'He should have asked *me* if he could take her!' Mrs Lisle wailed in protest.

'Yes, perhaps, but you must excuse him. He's used to referring to me. And anyway, wasn't it in fact Gina who took *him*, and in our experience Gina rarely asks leave of anyone?' Cabot asked drily of Danielle, who agreed with a nod.

'But that's terrible! What did I—I mean you'—Beatrix Lisle corrected hastily—'send her to that expensive school for, if not for her to learn good manners? And that lad! Have you really let them run around together like a couple of guttersnipes? My friends, the—the people I want her to know, won't care for that—won't understand it *at all.*'

Cabot defended Simon calmly. 'Simon Milward is a little older than Gina. He's balanced, dedicated to learning his job and entirely responsible to me. There's not much Gina can learn from him that she doesn't know already, but she won't have him as an escort for much longer. He'll be coming back to England when I go, and after that she'll be all yours, for remodelling as you wish.'

'Yes,' Mrs Lisle agreed faintly. 'We've got to talk about that.'

'We have indeed,' said Cabot. At which Felipe discreetly excused himself, and Danielle would have done the same if Cabot hadn't said, 'No, you're in on this', as he might have done if they were really engaged.

Mrs Lisle complained, 'You see, I had plans for Gina. Nice friends who want to know her, one in particular, a charming young man of such good family, so eligible——'

'Eligible for what?' Cabot broke in.

'Why, for marriage, of course!'

'Is he rich? What does he do? How old is he?'

'Oh, he has money—at least, his family has. Do? You mean, what's his job? Well, nothing very definite. He introduces clients to his father's wine-shipping business, and he has racing connections. His name is Franchot Busier, and he's about thirty-five. He thinks he could entertain more successfully if he were married and he's been looking forward to meeting Gina. But she's such a shock—so gauche, so raw!'

Cabot agreed, 'She's certainly not cooked to a turn for immediate betrothal to a thirty-five-year-old playboy. But what did you expect? A charm-school trained debutante, curtsey and all? My dear Beatrix, teenagers don't come that way any more, and if you want her so, you'll have to school her yourself for quite a long time.'

Pale blue eyes widened in dismay. 'But I can't afford to keep her! I can only just get by as it is.'

'Then you must find her a job, or she must train for something where she'll be paid while she's being trained. You cannot and shall not try to buy her a meal ticket—and perhaps one for yourself too—by marrying her off to a man twice her age who wants a hostess for his table. Not that she'd adorn any table for graciousness or tact at the moment, as I'm sure your Monsieur Busier would agree at sight. So what have you got to lose?'

Cabot's tone had lightened from the hard authority with which he had issued his veto. But Gina's mother was not mollified.

'How dare you suggest I'm selling her for money?' she demanded.

'On your own showing——' Cabot murmured.

'Yes, well—she is *my* daughter, and of marriageable age!'

'Which is a pity for her, with a mother like you.

However, I'll send her to stay with you, and you must get to know each other and sort yourselves out as best you can.'

Cabot had risen and Mrs Lisle got up too. 'I never thought you could be so hardbitten and pitiless,' she accused him, and turned to Danielle. 'You've chosen a monster of intolerance for a husband, my dear. A monster, no less,' she said with almost pleasurable malice. And then, 'I'd like to get my wrap. Will you show me where?'

'Goodnight, Beatrix.' Cabot shook her hand without offering to escort her. Danielle had Suli call a taxi for her and saw her into it before she returned to the saloon. Cabot, Scotch in hand, was leaning against the ornate mantel which was the focal point of the room. He gestured towards the drinks cabinet, but she shook her head. She didn't know how to take his attitude over Gina. He had made his *diktat*, 'You cannot and shall not . . .' but he had offered himself to deliver Gina to the enemy camp. Where did he really stand?

Danielle said slowly, 'You're sending Gina to live with her mother as you planned. But supposing she can work on Gina's feeling for her to the point where Gina might give in and agree to this marriage? What then?'

Cabot shook his head. 'When Gina becomes as biddable as that, that'll be the day. Besides, if Beatrix has painted her as a fragile piece of Dresden china, this Busier guy is going to have the shock of his life, wouldn't you say?'

Danielle smiled wryly. 'Yes. So you think there isn't any danger Mrs Lisle could get her way? But suppose there *were*—danger, I mean—what would you do? What could you do? You and Gina aren't even related.'

Cabot drained his glass and set it down. 'Gina—promised in marriage against her will at sixteen, to this chap or any other Beatrix Lisle can lure into her web?'

'Yes——'

'Over my dead body,' he said.

If he had been any other man Danielle might have hugged him for that. For momentarily she—almost—loved him.

CHAPTER EIGHT

THERE was no word from Gina for several days. Then the telephone calls began. As Cabot and Felipe were ashore all day at their conference, the burden of answering these mostly fell on Danielle.

What was she supposed to be *doing*? Gina wanted to know. Her mother spent most of the time playing bridge, taking guitar lessons, ('she hasn't a clue') and window-shopping at Yves St Laurent and Cardin for things she couldn't afford.

'I'm mostly in the kitchen with her *bonne*, who at least is teaching me French. But twiddling my thumbs with a servant isn't all hilarious fun, and if I go out, or for a swim, Mother seems afraid I shan't come back, which some time I mightn't, at that,' Gina claimed.

'Have you met any of her friends?' Danielle asked.

'Yes, some. Beady-eyed Frenchwomen who examine me and practically turn me over to see if I look any better on the other side, as they would a joint of meat. One of them with a middle-aged son who came with her—imagine, to a women's tea-party!—and who, judging by Mother's questions as to what I thought of him, is what they call *un bon parti*—a good match for a girl, the girl being me.'

'And what did you think of him?' Danielle asked.

'As wet as they come. Impossible. Look, couldn't we make a date for one of the concerts we saw advertised? And where's Simon? May I talk to him?'

But Simon on that occasion was at the Convention Centre with Cabot, and Cabot discouraged more contact with Gina than necessary.

'I've got to give Beatrix enough rope to hang herself, and to be fair, Gina has got to try,' he ruled, and Danielle saw his point.

Louise had rejoined *Pandora* after three days in St Tropez, and with her arrival the yacht's social pace quickened. On any evening when Cabot was not entertaining business colleagues, she needed to be escorted to the gaming tables of the Casino, or to dinner at the Hotel de Café or the Hermitage, and she was able to spend her days, not window shopping at the *hautes couturiers*, but being fêted in their salons.

She affected to be surprised that Danielle did not shop as extravagantly as she did herself. 'Carlos is rich, but Cabot is *rolling* in money.' And her meeting with her English friends in St Tropez had further whetted her curiosity about Cabot's and Danielle's romance—about a past which it hadn't had, and about a future it wasn't going to know.

'As you aren't going on to Paris, as I am, I wonder you don't order your trousseau here? Where do you plan to marry, by the way? Out here, now Cabot has got rid of Gina, or is he going to make you face all the brouhaha there's going to be in England?' she probed.

Danielle parried that with the truth that they would be returning to England before anything was settled. Whereupon Louise mused, 'You'd hardly believe, would you, that according to the English people I was with in St Tropez, Cabot's confidential secretary is supposed to have said he'd never mentioned any fiancée to her, and that when she finalised the arrangements for this cruise, the only guests he proposed to bring along were Felipe, Gina and myself?'

Danielle found an answer to that too. 'Well, that's understandable,' she said. 'His announcement in *The Times* was the first publicity our engagement had. That was made only the day before we sailed, and he only decided to bring me along because he knew the Press would feel cheated of follow-up news and probably wouldn't leave me alone.'

'All the same, you'd think his *secretary*——?'

'Would know all about it?' Danielle prompted. 'Well, perhaps she did, but Cabot may have warned her that the best way to keep the newshunters off her back was to play dumb monkey and know nothing. But if you're really curious,' she added with a touch of malice, 'why don't you ask him how much anyone in England knew or didn't know about our plans before we sailed?'

At that Louise shrugged. 'Oh, it doesn't matter,' she said. 'It was just that, knowing just how *close* Cabot and I have always been, these people expected me to know all about his latest girl-friend, only to find themselves disappointed,' Which Danielle recognised as a mask for Louise's own disappointment in failing to learn the more which she had hoped to be able to pass on.

Unfortunately Danielle's satisfaction at having skirted that particular hazard was to be short-lived, when, a few days later, chance sponsored a meeting between Louise and someone hitherto unknown to them both.

Danielle was leaving the yacht one afternoon when she heard herself accosted in English. The voice came from a young man at the foot of the gangway, saying, 'Excuse me, but could you tell me whether a Miss Gina Lisle is aboard?'

Danielle shook her head. 'I'm afraid not. Who wants her?' she asked.

'I do.'

'And you are——?'

'A friend of hers. That is, sort of. My name is Colin Hunter, and we——' he smiled ingenuously—'well, we rather picked each other up on the Rock of Gibraltar, and I gave her a phone number here where she could call me. But she hasn't, and——'

Colin Hunter. *Colin Hunter?* Danielle searched her memory for the name and found it. Of course! The young freelance whose curiosity about herself and Cabot had so offended Gina that she had snubbed him roundly and had promised him nothing. Guessing Gina would only thank her for getting rid of him, Danielle said sharply,

'Yes, I remember Gina told us about you. But she isn't here. That is, she's left the yacht now, and I don't think she would want to see you if she hadn't, Mr Hunter.'

His jaw set mulishly. 'You can't know that. She took my phone number!'

'But didn't keep it, or mean to.'

'Well, where *is* she now? She was cruising in this yacht with Mr Steele, wasn't she? That's where I knew I could find her.'

'But you won't, I'm afraid. She's ashore in the city and won't be coming back. And if she'd wanted to get in touch with you, she'd have done so, I'm sure. I'm sorry, Mr Hunter——' Danielle turned her back on him, leaving him standing. When she looked back he hadn't moved, but as, even if he questioned the crew, he could only get the answer that Gina had left the yacht, she didn't worry that Gina would hear any more of him. There, however, she hadn't reckoned with Louise's greed for information, given and received and conned over for possible use.

Louise attacked that evening when the men had gone ashore to a stag dinner at the Convention Centre. Casually she remarked, 'By the way, that scoop-hunting young man Gina met on the Rock turned up here this afternoon, looking for her. He was being rather persistent with the deck steward, so I took him in hand to tell him she was living with her mother in the city, though as I didn't know the address, I couldn't help him.'

So I didn't satisfy him, thought Danielle. 'That was just as well,' she told Louise guardedly. 'Because I'm sure Gina wouldn't want to see him. You may remember she told us she resented his being too snoopy altogether.'

'Though this time he had quite as much to tell as to ask,' Louise murmured. 'For he had *the* most extraordinary story which he swore was true, having got it straight from the girl herself, who'd kept it to herself until then, as nobody would believe her, she was sure. She wouldn't tell him at first, but he took her out for the evening, gave her a few drinks, and when she opened up, there it was.'

Danielle's heart missed a beat. 'What was? And what girl was this?' she asked.

Louise snapped impatient finger and thumb. 'Oh—— Carol?—— Carmen somebody?—— what does it matter? Anyway, Cabot's secretary, the one who——'

'And what was the story?' Danielle pressed.

'Why, about Cabot and you! This Carol whoever told the Hunter boy she was quite certain—you're going to enjoy this!—that when Cabot had advertised for a working hostess for *Pandora*, it was a Miss Kane, whom she herself had shown into his office—a complete stranger to them both—who'd got the job!' As she stopped speaking Louise's eyes looked bright with mischievous expectancy of Danielle's scorn or denial or both.

But Danielle, completely thrown for the moment, could only manage an inviting 'And——?' which seemed to take Louise aback in her turn.

'*And*?' she echoed. 'Then you—you admit the girl was right? You were that Miss Kane? You *were* only hired by Cabot to run the domestic show on this trip? You didn't meet each other in America or get engaged there or anywhere else? You *are* just a common hireling of Cabot's; making fools of us all, the public; conning my husband and Felipe and me and our friends that you and Cabot were happy-as-Larry lovers, when all the time——?' Louise's voice which had shrilled with righteous indignation deepened again to the growled threat of, '*Why?*'

Danielle, controlled again but now admittedly in the other woman's hands, confirmed quietly, 'We didn't meet in America. Our first encounter of any was when Cabot interviewed me for the job and offered it to me. We aren't lovers, but we've claimed an engagement—for our own good reasons, I may say; reasons which are of no concern to anyone else—the public, his friends, anyone at all.'

'No concern?' Louise echoed again. 'And "reasons"? Well, they'd better be good for a deception of this size, this utter *impertinence!*' she raged.

'They are, they were, I assure you. On both sides, but separate ones—Cabot had his, I had mine,' said Danielle.

'And Cabot's aside, not too difficult, I daresay, to guess at yours?' taunted Louise.

'Since you're not likely ever to learn what they were, perhaps you'd better guess?' Danielle invited.

'Easy. You'd *got* something on Cabot. Probably still have, or he wouldn't still be playing along with you. The engagement, our acceptance of you as an equal, the ring, the clothes—they were the price you demanded, the sum of your blackmail!' Louise crowed.

That wild shot proved conclusively to Danielle that, whatever were Cabot's real motives, Louise wasn't a party to his use of her. The thought gave a strange lift to her spirit and she managed a laugh.

'If you can't guess better than that, you should

ask Cabot to give you his side of the story,' she said.

'You're bluffing! But don't kid yourself that I shan't do that this very night, as soon as he gets back!'

'And then you can decide which version—mine, his or your own—you can pass on to your friend Hunter for his scoop, can't you?' But already Danielle was determined that it had to be from her, not from Louise, that Cabot must first hear that their masquerade was over. She wondered whether Louise saw the absurdity, as she did, of their both remaining where they were, like two female spiders with webs spread to catch the male, and as she doubted her ability to outsit Louise, she began to make plans for her escape.

In silence she returned to the book she had been reading, while Louise's needle stabbed savagely at a square of embroidery. Then, after some lapse of time, Danielle closed her book, stood, stretched, yawned elaborately and left the saloon in a credible show of being willing to leave the field to her enemy. She deplored the pretence that she was going to bed, but all was fair in love and war, and this *was* war.

She debated calling a taxi to take her to the Centre and having Cabot paged there, but decided instead to waylay him when he and Felipe and Simon left their hired car on the promenade opposite *Pandora*'s mooring. There was a café nearby where she could spend the time she might have to wait. In her cabin she changed from the long dress which might make her conspicuous, pulled a dark hood over her hair and left the yacht without being seen. In the café she sat at an unshaded window and was on her third black coffee when she judged it was time to go out to meet the car as it slowed for its parking.

She came into the beam of its headlights before they were switched off, and when the three alighted she pretended for the others' benefit that she had only just been dropped by her own taxi after visiting a Madame Tissot, an antique dealer with whom she had made friends in her shop. 'It's a lovely night,' she claimed as Cabot's hand went beneath her elbow, and then in an undertone to him, 'Don't go aboard—I have to see you. Make some excuse.'

He looked surprised, but took his cue from her urgency. 'A drive? Good idea,' he said, and turned back to the car. 'Where would you like to go?'

As they drove off, Danielle realised that with the other two's arrival in the saloon minus Cabot, Louise must realise she had been foiled. But that couldn't be helped. There was too much at stake.

Without consulting her further, Cabot drove up through the Old Town towards the Cathedral and the Royal Palace and drew up in the steeply terraced gardens near the magnificent Oceanic Museum. He switched off the headlights and turned to her. 'Now?' he questioned.

She hardly knew where to begin. 'Do you remember that freelance journalist who accosted Gina in Gib?' she asked. 'Well, he turned up today, looking for her. I told him she wasn't on board any more and wouldn't want to see him. But he caught Louise later and told her the story he hopes to sell to the English papers.'

'What story?'

'Our story. He had heard from your secretary—

who would be the girl who showed me in for my interview with you——?'

Cabot nodded. 'A rather upstage temp. My confidential girl was on holiday.'

'Yes, well, this man Hunter had talked to this girl, who told him that "Danielle Kane" was just one of the people who had answered your advertisement, and that she'd got the job.'

'And so?'

'Don't you see? Louise confirmed for him what he already suspected—for there to be two Miss Kanes, one engaged to you and one who applied for a job, was too much of a coincidence, and therefore your account of having met me in America must be a plant, and the Miss Kane whom you brought on this trip was no more than a hired help——'

'Just a minute,' Cabot cut in. 'Paper over the meeting in America bit, and why need there *be* two of you? Why couldn't I have hired a Miss Kane to do a job, and have fallen in love with her and proposed to her before we sailed?'

'Because you didn't, that's why,' Danielle retorted.

'Who's to know that? And I distinctly remember——'

Danielle snapped, 'Louise knows, for one. She's pumped me for details about our affair. And you didn't propose before we sailed. You made conditions, and I agreed to them.'

'That's hair-splitting. But how have you learned all this?'

'From Louise, of course. She sent the young man away with enough notoriety slotted into place to fill columns. She's furious about our deception of her——'

'You've admitted it, then?'

'I had to, and though I didn't oblige her with our reasons, she claimed she could guess at them.'

'H'm, it's none of her clairvoyant business, but what does she suppose they were?'

'She suggested I had cause to—to blackmail you, and my price was this fake engagement with all the trimmings. I didn't disillusion her. At the time I was glad she could be so far out, but since then I've been thinking—— I mean, mightn't we be wise to let her and everyone believe she's right?'

Danielle met Cabot's eyes, cold as marbles. 'Wise? *Right*?' he exploded. 'To brand me publicly as a victim of blackmail, and you with the power to threaten me? You must be mad!'

How could she have foreseen his anger would be for the slur on himself for suffering menace at any woman's hands? But that was the supreme insolence of his pride. She shook her head. 'It could be the way out,' she persisted. 'You could admit to Louise it was all my doing for the reason she thought. That should put her on your side. And I—I could just disappear from the scene.'

'And you imagine you'd be allowed to disappear, with blackmail as a cause of the hoax to which I've been a party? Why, it would be the scoop of the year,' Cabot sneered. 'No, we have to get in first with the truth——'

'We haven't *got* any truth to tell,' she said bitterly.

'You think not?' His tone was quieter now. 'And what is *Pandora*'s radio for, if it's not to be used tonight to give Fleet Street a firm date and place for our marriage—out here and as soon as we can lay it on?'

Danielle's sharp-drawn breath was of dismay that he could believe he could deal with this crisis with yet more lies. 'You really think you can smother one hoax by concocting a bigger one? A date and place for our marriage! Now it's *you* who must be mad!' she scorned.

'Never more sane, as you'll come to allow, I know. Listen—how's this? I fell in love at first sight when I thought I was only hiring a hostess for *Pandora*. The meeting in America bit—a cover for your blushes against any nasty suggestions of a shotgun affair. The cruise—the escape from publicity which we claimed for it, and a getting-to-know-each-other-on-the-way. The rest—a teasing of the columnists until our plans were set, but now that they are, every man jack of them can enter up the date in his diary and bring his photographers along. What's wrong with that for a disarming story that's going to take the engagement to its logical conclusion?'

Danielle sighed in despair. 'Nothing,' she said wearily, 'except that the final lie, being the biggest, is going to blow up in our faces with a louder bang than the rest. There's going to be no marriage for any journalist to report, as you must know very well.'

'On the contrary.' She watched in fascinated horror as he took a diary from an inside pocket and flicked its leaves. 'How would the English Church below the Casino Gardens, and, say, Wednesday the seventeenth suit you? Could you be ready?'

'Ready?' she echoed stupidly. 'But you can't mean——? You don't—— We aren't——' She stopped in bewildered confusion.

Cabot took her up. 'Agreed, we aren't in any usual engaged situation. We're in a jam, from which we can only escape by way of a marriage that will scotch any suspicion that we've been acting a lie all along. So we strangle it at source— namely Louise—by going back now to announce our plans, and I doubt if she'll dare to challenge them.'

'You're saying you'd go through with it?' Danielle hesitated.

'Marriage takes two,' he said meaningly. 'But yes—there has to be a public ceremony to convince our friends—and our enemies—that there's been no hoax and we've meant business all along. What do you say?'

'To that kind of travesty—worse than any lie we've acted yet? No!'

'No? Yet a few minutes ago you were ready to be hounded as a common blackmailer. Would marriage to me be so much worse a fate than that?' he insinuated.

'It wouldn't be a real marriage!'

'Which is where you're wrong. I'm a man of my word; I've played the field and enjoyed women——'

'Louise among them!' she flashed.

'Louise when she was single,' he confirmed. 'But I offered none of them marriage, and now I do offer it to you, I expect it to be honoured—in every way. You understand me?'

She did, only too well. He would lend her his

name and a share in his status and his wealth. They
would show a bright, conventional face to their
world and keep another for their private hours—
hers, frustrated and love-starved; his, arrogantly
possessive of a wife he would use but wouldn't
value. And yet if only he knew her true motive in
agreeing to their pact, what right had she to expect
him to value her?

She had always thought that the final scene between them would be the one in which she would
fling at him the defiance of why she had taken and
spent his money, accepted his ring and enjoyed
equality with his guests—for the sole purpose of
avenging her aunt's unnecessary death in the only
way open to her. In her mind's many rehearsals,
she had gloried in the telling, so why, in the face of
his quixotic offer of marriage, should the savour
have gone out of it, turning her story, if it were
ever told, into a confession, instead of the heady
triumph it should have been?

She had no answer to that. She only knew that
the force behind her revenge had petered out like a
spent engine, that the story had to be confession
and that the moment for it was now.

'I understand,' she told him, and then, 'But
there's something I have to tell you before we go
any farther in—all this.'

'Something that affects it?'

'About myself, yes.'

'Go on.' He waited in silence while she sought
for words which wouldn't come. But she *had* to
find them. Hesitantly she began, 'It goes back to
the day you offered me the job and I took it——
Or no, it goes back farther still——'

The telling came more freely after that, but without the bitter accusations she had rehearsed so often. It became a deadpan account of her connection with a certain terrace of Georgian houses in Putney which had fallen victim to the bulldozers of Cabot Steele; of the woman who had held out in vain to the brink of poverty; of her death for which her niece had held Cabot Steele morally responsible, and of that niece's snatch at the chance to avenge it.

'You may have thought I just gave in weakly to your conditions,' Danielle finished, 'but it wasn't so at all. I asked for an absurdly huge salary and determined to take you for any amount of money you cared to spend on me, and promised myself that when we parted you were going to hear why I'd done it. So that's why I'm telling you now.'

Though it lasted for less than a minute the silence which followed seemed endless. Then Cabot said reflectively, 'I see. And I remember the project of the Terrace Adelaide quite well. But as we aren't parting, why air your grievance about it now?'

She saw that as studiedly callous. 'It wasn't just a grievance,' she protested. 'It was a——'

He nodded. 'All right. To you it was a kind of sacred crusade. Is it still?'

No explanations. No justification for the rape of people's homes, their livelihoods, their futures. Just this detached acceptance of her story as if it had nothing to do with him! He put his question again. 'Is it still?'

She remembered her realisation that it wasn't. 'No,' she said. 'Not any longer.'

Again thoughtfully, he said, 'I wonder why not? But if not, why bring it up now?'

Surely he must know? 'Because,' she faltered, 'knowing this about me, you can't possibly think of marrying me just to shield me from the notoriety of our hoax!'

'My dear girl'—his tone was pseudo-patient, not affectionate, 'you flatter yourself if you imagine I'm not shielding myself from notoriety too. We're in this together and your motives for joining me in it aren't of the slightest importance to the issue, which is that we let Louise and her journalist make all the nasty capital they can out of her story, or we marry on the seventeenth.' He paused. 'May I take it you're persuaded it's the only way?'

She gave in. 'I—suppose so.'

'No hidden motives this time?'

'No.'

She dreaded his saying anything as banal as, 'Good', or pressing on her the mockery of a kiss. But he did neither. He switched on his headlights, revved his engine and looked at his watch. 'We ought to be able to make tomorrow's later editions in Fleet Street,' he said, and set the car to the sweep down to the yacht harbour and the dazzle of the night-lit city.

He took her with him when he went to the radio room to dictate his message for London. Then he collected Captain Fortescue and the First Officer for a gathering in the saloon with Louise and the men. He rang to the galley for champagne to be taken off ice, and with an arm round Danielle's waist, announced his news.

'The moment I hope you've all been waiting for,'

he said. 'We've decided to give the local reporters a whirl by getting married here on the seventeenth. You thought we were never going to get around to it, didn't you? Well, just how wrong can you get?'

There was a buzz of interest and a clamour of congratulations to him which Danielle scarcely heard as she watched for Louise's reaction. She felt Louise would not allow herself to show surprise, but could she possibly pretend to pleasure? What would she say . . . do? Trembling, her thigh hard-pressed against Cabot's for confidence, Danielle waited, and knew he was tensed too.

Her smile thin, Louise said in a light throwaway tone, 'We certainly weren't expecting it, and I think even Danielle supposed she would still be single when she went back to England, a lot richer in the experience of being engaged, but with marriage still in front of her, not behind. *One* of you must have been very impatient, and of course we can guess which—— As for you, Cabot——' she turned to him—'it's really too bad of you to cheat your loyal English public of the end to the Steele–Kane elopement story. They deserve better than that!'

Danielle breathed again and felt Cabot relax. Nobody who didn't understand the malice behind Louise's words could read anything offensive into their raillery. For the moment at least, Louise had accepted defeat and had weakened her case by failing to denounce Danielle as a successful black-mailer then and there to the others. Later she would find it difficult to explain her forbearance, and Danielle sensed that Cabot knew her claws had been drawn.

He said, 'They don't need my pity. By the time

we get back home, the gossip boys will probably have another clutch of stories about us—that we parted on our wedding night and have been reunited, or that Danielle has been seen dining tête-à-tête with a boy-friend, putting our marriage again on the rocks——' He moved away to hand round the champagne which the steward was pouring. Giving Louise her glass, he said, 'What a pity you and Felipe are off so soon. When do you go? The day after tomorrow? Oh, couldn't you postpone Paris, so that you could be here for the wedding?'

She shook her head. 'If you'd wanted us here, you could have given us longer notice, I'd have thought. But of course it was a *snap* decision, wasn't it—just made tonight?' She looked across at Felipe. 'We can't stay, can we?' she asked, but smothered his half-willing, 'Well——' with a decisive 'No, we must leave as we planned. We can look forward to seeing you both in Lisbon some time later on. Perhaps?'

Her tiny pause before the last word made a doubt of it, but Cabot ignored its meaning and moved on.

At Danielle's side again, 'We must let Gina know,' he told her. 'Would you like to fetch her here for the day tomorrow?'

Danielle half turned her back on the others. 'Could we leave it until Louise and Felipe have gone?' she asked in an undertone.

'Still afraid of the lady's tongue?' he murmured back. 'I think you needn't be. She wouldn't have let the boy loose with his scoop until she'd sounded you out, and with our story splashed all over the English papers tomorrow morning, he's going to

be too late to find a home for his, even if she hasn't
the good sense to tell him to kill it. Easy.'

Easy! If only it were! Everything was moving too
fast for Danielle. Now it was Gina who would be
expected to accept this arranged marriage. As soon
as the news was out, there would be a barrage of
reporters' questions, she supposed, and then—the
ceremony itself. While the others were talking, she
looked across the elegant saloon, grown familiar
and welcoming, at the man at whose wishes and
commands she was still dancing, puppet-like and
mesmerised by his manipulation of her. Or—her
thought suddenly doubted—was she still blindly
captive and struggling, or was her present submission to him a willing surrender stemming from a
need to be at one with him, a hunger for him to
know her, not as his fellow trickster or his catspaw,
but as she really was?

The unbidden doubt had surprised her, but she
knew the answer was yes. With her confession to
him she had become her own woman again. Free.
Free to act at her own will. Free to try to be for
one man whatever he wanted of her. Free—to
love.

From her watching of Cabot, arrogant of profile
and magnificently male, she looked at the facets of
light caught in the celebratory glass of wine she
held, and down at the ring he had entrusted to her
good faith in their pact, now the symbol of the
promise of his future to her.

And felt her brief euphoria slip away. *She* could
love him . . . knew now for certain that she did.
But he? What did he even pretend he had for her?
Nothing. This marriage of convenience for them

both which he had warned her would be 'real', would have a veneer of the qualities marriage should have, but with love on only one side—hers—it would have no warmth, no heart, no delight.

How was she going to bear it? *How?*

CHAPTER NINE

OVERNIGHT, when the party in the saloon had broken up, Danielle had hoped that Cabot would come to her room, and she had not undressed until she had heard his own door close upon him. This had surprised and hurt her. He had given her no indication of his personal reaction to her confession, and so much else remained unspoken between them—two people who proposed to link their lives in a few days' time. She wondered whether, as punishment for her story, he meant to ostracise her in private, however attentive he had to appear in public. He couldn't ignore her completely when they were alone; if nothing else, there must be talk of plans and arrangements, but last night she had hoped for some understanding, some tenderness, in return for her surrender to his purpose. If he had tempted her to it, she would have been ready with as much outgiving passion as she had had to deny herself before. But he had not asked it of her, and his silence showed he could not pretend to it himself.

Meanwhile, after hours of fitful sleeping and waking, there was the day to be faced, Cabot to be encountered in public, and in private, Louise to be avoided as far as possible, and the leisurely shipboard routine to be followed.

In expecting this latter, however, Danielle found she was wrong. Cabot had already been busy, discussing with Captain Fortescue the ways and means of the wedding breakfast's being given in the yacht. She would be dressed overall; a chef from the Hotel de Paris would be put in charge of the catering; a professional hostess would handle all the other hospitalities.

'There'll be no need for you to trouble yourself about a thing,' he told Danielle in Louise's hearing. 'Your only duty will be to sweep up the aisle in the most alluring creation Dior can produce——' Standing just behind her chair as he spoke, he dropped a kiss on her hair, and smoothed it before he moved away.

Impulsively she caught at his hand as he passed her. It was a mute gesture of appeal which she hoped he would understand. But there was nothing in his expression which seemed to promise he had.

Escaping Louise was easier than she had feared. Possibly Louise, vindictive still but compelled to silence, was equally anxious to avoid her? Whether or not, she made considerable business out of packing for herself and Felipe, and they both spent most of the day in the city, making last calls on people they had met and confirming their next morning's flight to Paris. Danielle had feared that, for show's sake, Cabot would suggest taking them out for a farewell dinner, but he did not, and her only encounter alone with Louise was in the saloon before the men joined them for the evening aperitif. The usual sheaf of the English morning papers had just arrived by air, and Louise had one of the popular tabloids spread open for reading when Danielle went in.

Louise closed the paper and threw it aside. 'I see Carson Carson'—naming Fleet Street's most notorious columnist—'has done you proud,' she sneered. 'I suppose the rest have done the same.'

Danielle thought, *This can't last long. I must keep my cool.* 'Cabot will be pleased,' she said. 'He'd have been disappointed if they'd forgotten us and our private affairs after all these weeks.'

'Well, *you've* nothing to be disappointed over, have you?' Louise challenged. 'You've played your cards pretty well, I must say. You're exactly where you meant to be, and no one with a clue about how you did it.'

All innocence, 'Did what?' Danielle asked.

'Landed a prize like Cabot Steele, apparently without even trying, of course. Considering how he managed to conduct his amours without having to commit matrimony to date, and the hush-hush way he whisked you out of London, there were bound to be rumours that you'd got some hold over him, and that he was putting you off with an open-ended engagement while he thought his way out of it. You know how people talk.'

This sounded as if Louise were conceding victory with however little grace, and Danielle decided to meet her halfway. 'Yes indeed,' she agreed. 'But as long as the talk has had to stop at mere rumour, what harm has been done?'

Their eyes met, Danielle's in candid question, Louise's in sullen defeat. 'You can't help people *wondering*,' she muttered. But there was no threat in her tone. As a menace she was finished.

The next day, when Danielle and Cabot had seen Felipe and Louise off from Nice airport, he suggested they should go together to fetch Gina to the yacht, though he hadn't warned either her or her mother that they were coming, he said.

At the apartment the door was opened to them by Mrs Lisle's *bonne*, the general maid with whom Gina had said she spent most of her time.

'Madame? Yes—But yes, she is at home,' the girl faltered in French. 'She is, however, much worried, you understand, about Mademoiselle Gina, who——' She broke off there as Mrs Lisle appeared at the door of the living-room and hurried forward at sight of Cabot.

The maid effaced herself. Cabot began, 'Where's Gina? We came to take her down to *Pandora* for the day——' But Gina's mother had him by the slack of his shirt and was shaking him in agitation.

'*Gina*?' she shrilled. 'She's not here! Don't *you* know where she is? If not, why not? And if not, *where has she gone*?'

Cabot gently detached his shirt from the clutching fingers. 'Are you saying, Beatrix, that Gina isn't just out; that she's gone somewhere, without telling you or your *bonne* where?'

Beatrix Lisle gritted her teeth in exasperation. 'But of *course* that's what I'm telling you! She's *left*, this morning, taking all her things. Her room is empty, and all we found in it was a note saying—— Come in, and you can read it for yourselves.'

They followed her into the living-room where she handed him a sheet of paper, from which he read aloud to Danielle:

'I'm leaving. When I get to where I'm going I'll write to you and tell you. But don't try to fetch me, because I'm not coming back.'

Danielle caught a breath of dismay and Cabot

turned to Mrs Lisle. 'Can't you explain this? Has she been seeing anyone not known to you—male or female? Or have any letters come for her here?'

Beatrix pouted. 'No one has been here for her while I've been at home. But how do I know who she may have been meeting while she's been out? Letters? Yes, she has had one or two. What? Local or from England? *I* don't know. I don't collect stamps; I wouldn't have looked at the envelopes.'

'Did she have enough money to get far afield?'

'She had some, I daresay. I don't know how much.'

'And you can't explain why she's chosen to go just now, considering the talks you and I have been having about her?' Cabot explained to Danielle, 'I hadn't told you, darling, but Beatrix and I have been discussing Gina's future. I've suggested that if Beatrix will agree to let her go back to England with us, I'll make myself responsible for her getting as much more education as she needs to go to college or train for a job. Back to boarding school for her A-levels first, of course. She can spend her vacations with us.' As if at a sudden thought he turned back to Beatrix. 'You'll have told her about this, I'm sure?'

Beatrix moved uncomfortably. 'No.'

'*No*?' he rasped. 'Why not?'

'It's no concern of hers while I haven't agreed.'

'It's of prime concern to her. It's her youth, her life,' Cabot snapped. 'You've got to give her the right to accept or refuse my offer, and if she relished the alternative you've been putting to her, would she have run away?'

'She's a silly girl who doesn't know what's good for her.'

'She's a stubborn wench with a mind of her own,' Cabot retorted. 'You know perfectly well which way she'll jump, given the choice you've kept from her. You've hardly seen her since her father died; you don't want her for herself—only as a means to keeping you in the state to which you've been accustomed, as the saying goes, and since she's shown she isn't standing for that, and I'm not either, I think you'd better agree to my proposals, don't you?'

'You're hard. Everything is so expensive, and I'm always overspent,' Beatrix wailed. 'I have to do what I can to get by.'

'As long as what you "can" doesn't include selling your daughter, as a one-off operation I'll settle your current bills,' Cabot promised.

'But how am I to manage in the future if she doesn't marry well?'

Cabot moved towards the door, gesturing to Danielle. 'You could try working for your living. You'd be surprised how it helps with the bills,' he said.

Beatrix followed them to the open door of the apartment. 'But what about Gina? What do I do?'

'If you've really no idea where she may have gone, there's nothing you can do. I'll think of ways of tracing her, and keep you posted. Meanwhile you could steady your nerves by reading the Situations Vacant columns in *Nice-Matin*. When Gina shows up you could be needing one of them, because she'll be coming back to England with us.'

'I'm her *mother*!'

Cabot was handing Danielle into the car. 'That's her handicap,' he told Beatrix over his shoulder. 'For the next year or two, until she comes of age, she'll have to make do with a godfather instead.'

Before they moved off Danielle said, 'You were very harsh with her.'

'No more so than she can take. She's equipped with inbuilt armour against criticism or blame. I've been working on her for days—for too long, using the soft touch with no result until now.' Cabot thumped the steering wheel with both hands and stared ahead. 'I was bluffing, of course, that I might only have to shout, 'Hi! You there!' and Gina would come running. In fact, I haven't a clue where to look for her. Have you?'

Glad as she was that he should appeal to her, Danielle could only shake her head, and offer, 'If she didn't leave until this morning, she can't have got far.'

'She could have taken a bus or train or plane. It depends what money she had.'

'If she had enough, do you suppose she could be making for England by herself?'

'She couldn't—or only with difficulty. I've still got her passport in *Pandora*'s safe.'

'Oh.' Danielle thought for a moment, then mused, 'From her note she seemed to be going somewhere definite, and she had had some letters ... *Nice-Matin* advertisements?—do you think she may have answered one about a job, and be going to it?'

Cabot agreed, 'Could be. But where?' He started the car. 'We must get back to *Pandora* and see if she's thrown us a passing thought on her way.'

Us. As always, in speaking of himself and her,

he used the word with the same ease with which he scattered small endearments to her. As if they were any ordinarily happy couple within a few days of their marriage, when he was as fully aware as she of the mockery they were enacting! She envied him his ability to dissemble, wished she could do the same—except that any endearments she dared offer him would be real, meant, heartfelt. And he wouldn't know the difference . . . wouldn't care, even after marriage, whether there were any, as long as their façade of harmony was intact.

Neither of them expected there to be any news of Gina at the yacht. To run there from her mother's apartment would have been too obvious. She must have made other plans.

There was further annoyance for Cabot in finding that Simon was not on board. 'He has no business to leave in the middle of a working morning,' Cabot chafed irritably. 'I'd thought to send him round the bus stops and to the station, while I do the police and the airport with Gina's description. As neither Dora nor her maid had seen her today, we don't know what she was wearing. How do you suppose she'd have dressed for a journey?' he asked Danielle, who said ruefully,

'Probably in teenage uniform—sandals and dungarees, and she'd have a backpack for her things. Though if she were going straight to a job, she may have made herself a bit more presentable. She does *have* a dress or two, I know.'

'Yes, well, stay here and man the phone, will you? I may want to ring back. Meanwhile, call Beatrix to tell her I'm putting enquiries in hand, and give Simon hell from me when he does deign to reappear.' As they were alone, there was no kiss or caress for Danielle from Cabot before he left.

She was still on the sundeck when, after a few minutes, he came back. 'Something I'd forgotten to see to in the office,' he explained. 'When you've rung Beatrix, you'd better park there, to be ready to answer the phone to me, or if we're rung from anywhere else.'

He was gone again before she made her call. She gave Gina's mother his message, did her best at optimism which she didn't feel herself, and promised to ring again the minute Cabot had news. Then, unable to think of anything but the problem of Gina, she sat down in Cabot's swivel chair, impatient of the emptiness of waiting for news which did not come.

Cabot kept an orderly desk. Big virgin blotter, an assortment of pens in a tortoiseshell stand, In tray, Out tray, dictaphone, manilla folders, a pile of the morning's mail as yet unopened, and beyond that a big English-stamped envelope which had been opened, its late contents in contrasting disarray, some of them about to slip to the floor.

Danielle reached to straighten them, saw they were a mixture of untouched black-and-white photographs and architectural drawings. As she squared them off for replacing, she looked them through. They seemed to be by way of 'Before' and 'After' impressions; the photos were of the dusty piled bricks and timbers of half-demolished buildings, the drawings, neat delicately lined sketches of façades—a public house with its forecourt and hanging sign, a complex of two-storeyed apartments, an office block, a crescent of a dozen or so private houses, small, beautifully proportioned ... and utterly familiar.

Sketched to each attached house was its low broad step from the pavement, flanked by the wrought-iron handrails which it shared with its neighbours. Above each door was a crescent fanlight; there were ground-floor deep sash windows; narrow wrought-iron balconies to those on the first floor; above all, the parapet and steep slate roof which were typical of the period in which such a crescent of houses had been originally built. There was one exception to their uniformity. The middle house of the group had bow-fronted ground floor windows instead of sash, and it was this house which had pinpointed Danielle's recognition beyond all doubt ... the Terrace Adelaide, as it would have been nearly two centuries ago; as, more or less, except for vandalised bellpulls and broken windowpanes, it still had shabbily been before its violation which neither she nor Aunt Catherine had returned to witness.

The back of each photograph and sketch bore the rubber-stamped legend *Cabot Steele*, details of the subject and dates. The neat script on the back of the drawing in Danielle's hand read, *Terrace Adelaide, 1790, S. Putney. Scheduled for restoration to original design*—with a date a couple of months ahead.

Restoration? Danielle stared unseeingly across the office. That meant—that the Terrace would live again; that Cabot hadn't bought it to destroy, and if they had only known it wasn't to be reduced to mere rubble, she could have encouraged her aunt to live in hope they might return to it. But they hadn't known. Probably the decision to restore

hadn't been made until much later, and by then it
hadn't been the business of anyone in the huge
Cabot Steele consortium to seek them out and tell
them. Nobody's fault. Just Fate. Fate that Aunt
Catherine may have died too soon. Fate that
Danielle herself had nursed that canker of hatred
to the point where chance had stepped in to help
her, she had thought, to rid herself of its poison,
but had led her instead to her huge injustice to
Cabot, to whom she had finally confessed it, but
who hadn't denied it nor forgiven her. For if he
had, wouldn't he have helped her, eased her conscience, been—kind?

This marriage they had brought upon themselves—was it merely the necessity he claimed for
it, or did he mean to use it as her punishment,
tying her to——

She jumped with shock as the door opened and
Simon came in. 'Oh—you!' he panted at sight of
her. 'Where can I find the Chief? It's Gina!'

Danielle started up. '*Gina*? Where? You know?
She left home this morning without—— But she
got in touch with you? You've taken her back? Or
brought her back?'

'She wouldn't come. I've had to trick her.' Simon
was mechanically shuffling the pile of photos and
drawings into order. 'The Chief had left me to file
these things while you and he went to bring her
down, and I was doing it when she phoned on the
chance of getting me, not him, and told me I must
go to meet her at once, as she was in trouble.'

'Where was she then? Where is she now?'

'Was—is still—at the Italian border post. She
was making for San Remo, where she'd got a job

as an *au pair*. But she was put off the bus at the frontier, because she hadn't got either a passport or a card of entry, which the French and the Monegasques can get, so she rang me to take her passport to her, so that she could go on.'

'Which you couldn't do, of course?'

'Which I couldn't do, as it's in the safe with all ours,' Simon confirmed. 'But I pretended I could get it, and took the first taxi I could find. There she was, sitting on a road bollard and jumping with nerves lest I shouldn't come.'

'But when you told her you hadn't brought her passport?'

Simon grimaced. 'All hell broke loose! She hadn't realised she would need it, but what sort of a pal was I? Couldn't I have pretended I wanted some papers from the safe and borrowed the keys from the Chief? Or have been there when he opened it, and lifted the thing then? I told her nothing normal would be going on here. You and the Chief had gone to fetch her to spend the day, and you'd have heard she'd run away, which would have put you all in a flat spin, looking for her. If she wanted her passport, she would have to come back and ask for it herself, but if she took my advice she'd forget the whole thing.'

'And she wouldn't?'

'No. After a lot more argument I pretended to relent, and made her promise not to leave her bollard while I came back and tried again.'

'Did she believe you?'

'I wouldn't know. But as she couldn't go on and wouldn't come back, she hadn't much choice but to trust me. Not that I'd dare to show my face again without her passport in my fist. I have to hope the Chief will take over.'

'And he will,' Danielle promised. 'At present he's out in the city, making enquiries. But he'll be ringing back for news, or I may catch him at the police station.' As she took up the receiver she added, 'I don't think she'll refuse to come back with *him*. He has something to tell her that she'll be glad to hear.'

'Good,' said Simon. 'Though——' with a malicious grin—'What a pity about all this Riviera sun. A nice sharp English summer rain could work wonders of persuasion with someone sitting on a wet bollard for a whole morning and more! Meanwhile——' he indicated the envelope he was taking over to the file cabinet, 'you've been looking at these? They came by air from the architect's office last night. Interesting, aren't they?'

'Very,' said Danielle. 'Very,' and began her telephoning in a rather shaky voice.

Gina and Cabot did not come aboard until the evening. He had telephoned earlier that he was taking her out to lunch and for a godfatherly talk and then to her mother's apartment for them to make their peace with each other. This might be rather shattering for Gina, and would Danielle manage to keep Simon off-scene at first, as the kindest epithets Gina had had for him were 'twister' and 'double-crosser'? She would get over it, but while she had her knives out for him, it was better they be kept apart.

Simon thought so too, and was only too willing to dine with Captain Fortescue, leaving Danielle with mixed feelings—of relief over Gina and dread of Cabot's soulless reaction when she had to confess her new guilt to him. She had little hope it would clear any more between them than her first avowal of her distrust had done. He had ignored her humiliation over that, and would subject her to the same hard indifference now.

Gina did not appear much chastened by her escapade, but when she had gone to her cabin Cabot said, 'She's really as pleased as a monkey with two tails, but she needs to pay us out for dragging her back by the scruff of her neck when she thought she'd been clever. And though Beatrix wouldn't admit it, I suspect she was half-relieved to have her taken off her hands.'

'What about the people who were expecting Gina to go for the *au pair* job?' asked Danielle.

'I stood over her while she telephoned them. She'd lied to them about her age, and when they heard she was sixteen, not eighteen as she'd said, they didn't want to know either. But I'll be writing them an apology myself.' Cabot went to pour himself a drink. 'Not too many questions at dinner,' he advised. 'She's still licking her wounds.'

But as dinner progressed Gina's mood of truculence gradually softened. She admitted to looking forward to her future. She would go back to school and take A-levels and apply to go to veterinary college, and if Cabot really meant that she could spend her vacations with him and Danielle, she'd be grateful to do just that—when she wasn't doing anything else, of course, like pony-trekking or going to camp.

She refused coffee in the saloon after the meal. 'Where's Simon?' she demanded.

'He dined in the mess. He's probably still there,' Danielle told her.

Gina's eyes narrowed. 'Is he *afraid* of me?'

Danielle judged she could take some irony now. 'He's terrified,' she said.

'The daft ha'porth!' Gina snorted inelegantly. 'Did he really expect me to purr with delight when he promised to come back with my passport and sent Cabot instead? Let me get at him. I can hardly wait!'

Before they had finished their coffee she was back. 'We're going to the Disque d'Or. We may be late,' she announced from the doorway, and was gone again.

That left Cabot and Danielle to their first tête-à-tête evening she could remember. Cabot moved again. 'Let's go to the library,' he suggested. 'It's cosier for two.'

Cosy! For the little of chatty intimacy they had to share! But Danielle went along, bracing her nerves for the ordeal before her, wondering whether he would help her at all when he learned what she was telling him. She sat on the long settee facing the television screen, glad of its deep cushions billowing protectively round her. As Cabot took his seat at the far end he asked, 'Have you thought about your trousseau?'

She murmured non-committally, 'I don't need very much.'

'But the dress? You must go to one of the top salons.'

'Very well. But——'

'It promises to be a very big reception. If you put your ear to the ground you could probably hear the reporters pattering in already.'

'Oh.' She frowned in distress. 'Does it have to be like that? Couldn't——?'

'Wasn't it intended to be like that? Wasn't the bigger the better the object of the exercise for our purpose?'

'For *your* purpose.'

'For yours too. We were in harness.'

'But we needn't have been. You didn't have to shelter me. I'd been—using you. I *told* you—— And now——' She stopped, feeling as if a lot of taut threads inside her had suddenly snapped across and she had to go on without their support. She sat forward, hands between her knees, staring down, avoiding his eyes. 'And now, this morning, I learned that I'd wronged you hideously, misjudged you and had hated you before I knew you, without any cause. There were some papers strewn on your desk, photographs, drawings. There was one of—our terrace I'd blamed you for demolishing. But you hadn't. You've planned to restore it, *and I didn't know.*'

Cabot stirred, crossed his legs more easily. 'Good. So you found it,' he said mildly. 'I hoped you would.'

She lifted her head to stare at him. 'You knew it was there?'

'If you remember, I came back this morning. I'd forgotten to empty the envelope on my desk. I'd calculated you had enough of woman Eve in you to tempt you to investigate. Seems I was right.'

'You—you wanted me to know? Why didn't you tell me?'

'I had no idea you had any connection with Adelaide until the night you turned your conscience inside out, and then I thought its lining would do no harm for a little more airing before I let you tuck it back. But I never meant to bring you to the altar, hating me for the reasons you thought. For others enough, but not those. I wasn't guilty. They restored the façades of the Nash terraces in the Park, didn't they? So why not the Terrace Adelaide frontages, cracked drains, worm and wet rot notwithstanding—why not?'

Danielle forced a smile. 'By courtesy of Cabot Steele—why not?' she echoed tremulously.

'You don't deserve it, but you shall cut the ribbons when it's rebuilt. Sweetheart——' He had moved near enough to take her hand, but she wrenched free and huddled back among her cushions.

'Don't,' she begged. 'There's no one listening or watching. You don't have to pretend you feel any differently about me now than you ever did.'

'Nor do I. I haven't changed.'

'Exactly. I'm still the pawn I've always been for you to move about and control. You're frank at least!' she flashed.

'And honest.' The tawny eyes held hers. 'Listen—the story we've had ready for the gossips who ask—that my courtship of you was piratical because I'd fallen for you at first sight in my office and couldn't afford to let you go—was the truth as I've known it from that day. The rest, a chaperon for Gina, a hostess for the trip, a tame guide in port—they'd been the conditions of the job before you came along. After that, they were only the trimmings on my desperate need to keep you by me, near me, in sight. Do you remember my telling you that if you hadn't shown up, I'd have waited for you?'

'Which was nonsense.'

The corner of Cabot's mouth pulled upward. 'Odd. I thought it a piece of sound logic at the time.'

'It was flirtatious and silly. We—we weren't on those terms.' But her prim reproof was cover for a doubt, a bewilderment, a dawning hope which were fighting for expression but found none. She looked at Cabot in a dumb pleading for help.

'Yes?' he invited gently. 'What terms did you think we were on?'

Danielle found her tongue. 'Not those,' she said. 'Not flirtation nor banter. We were on the terms you'd laid down, which we'd both signed in black and white, and it wasn't fair of you to——'

'To tempt you beyond them?'

'Just for your pleasure, no.'

'And yet there were times—or at least one— when I thought it was for your pleasure as well as mine. Do you remember? And was I right?'

Bringing an aching tide of desire with it, her thought switched back to the night he meant. For pride's sake she ought to deny it, but she was beyond pride now, and she plunged deep into truth.

'Yes,' she said, 'I wanted you too.'

'I knew that,' he said with simple confidence. 'You were sweet with a passion you couldn't conceal; warm and answering and ready to give. But that didn't stop you from turning back to stone the next day, all haughty scorn of the poor fool

who'd aspired to you. What happened that night?'
he appealed. 'You said it wasn't Felipe's arrival.
Then what?'

'You'd claimed you meant nothing serious, and
suddenly I was ashamed to have any part in it.'

'On the very point of a surrender which would
have given you to me! I know I'd approached you
flippantly, but I was so sure of my body's speaking
urgently to yours that I was utterly shattered that
you should turn me down. I'd put all the passion I
had into making love to you. I thought you *must*
understand what it was telling you, and you seemed
to. But when you rejected it I called you by every
ugly name I knew, and I determined I wouldn't try
again that way.'

'But you wouldn't let me leave when I wanted
to.'

'I dared not. I couldn't risk seeing you turn your
back and walk out of my life. I threatened you in
order to keep you around, and it seemed to work.
But now I'm wondering whether you would have
stayed anyway, that you didn't really want to go?'

He had reached for her hand again, and this time
it stayed to clasp his and hold on. 'At that stage, if
you'd told me in so many words that you loved
me, you wouldn't have had to wonder,' she told
him softly. 'I *couldn't* have gone until the time came
for you to send me away.'

'Of which there was never any chance until I'd
asked you "in so many words" to love me in return
and to marry me.' Cabot paused. 'A pity we've
been shotgunned into marriage by Louise.
Wouldn't you have preferred a proposal to soft
music and an obliging moon?'

'*Have* I been proposed to?' Danielle asked mischievously.

'You have. Two nights ago, as I remember.'

'Did I say yes?'

'Under the coercion of my superior will, you did.'

'Then phooey to the moon and the music,' she crowed on a little gulp of ecstasy. 'If we've said yes to each other, what does anything else matter?'

'*I* said yes to you long ago,' Cabot claimed.

'And I to you—before I would admit it.' She moved towards him. 'Kiss me, please, Cabot—I want you to.'

'Oh, love—*love!*' They strained together, giving themselves up to the heady magic of touching and looking, finding special points of pleasure to caress—for Danielle the turn of Cabot's hard jaw; for him the soft hollow at the cleavage of her dress. He pressed her back into the depth of the cushions, his weight a burden to which her body moulded willingly, its pliancy the perfect complement to the hard male strength of his.

He held her off from him, his gaze, dark with passion, full of an urge to feast upon her looks. He kissed her gently, on the sensitive spot between her brows, on her eyelids, her ear tips, the point of her chin, her throat; avoiding her mouth until at last he took it in a great plunging assault which drew from her a long moan of delight. She exulted in knowing she had roused him to a high peak of desire for her, and as on that other night, she was responding with an abandonment of which he could ask anything, *anything* of her and she would give it. And not only give but take; her need was as great as his. And yet——

It was as if the nuance of her thought had reached him through some invisible antenna between them, for his searching hands stilled and he dragged his lips from hers to murmur. 'If I asked you to marry me *now*—you know what I mean by now?—would you?'

'Yes! Oh *yes*——'

'But? There's a "but" in your mind, isn't there? I can sense it. You would rather wait until we're on the far side of our eternal vows to each other—is that it?'

She nodded in dumb gratitude for his understanding. Then, 'How did you know?' she whispered. 'I—I'm sorry.'

'Don't be, my love. It's a brake you've a right to use, and I've served so much time for you already that I can hold out to possess you for a while longer.' He released her and settled himself easily beside her, still holding her hand. 'Talk to me instead. There's still a world of things to understand.'

They talked. Asked the age-old lovers' questions—'When did you first *know*?', 'Why did you pretend?', 'How could you be jealous?', 'Why were you afraid?' All the ice of their own pride's making melted in the sun of their avowals of love and trust and in their shared wonderment that so unique a magic as loving and being loved should have been worked for them.

They knew when Gina and Simon returned on board and heard them go to their cabins. Then Cabot stood and took Danielle into his arms for a goodnight kiss that lasted a very long time. 'Your last night in your cabin that's too close to mine for ny peace of of mind,' he told her. 'After we're married we'll move into the state suite for the journey home, but tomorrow you and Gina go to the Hotel de Paris until the wedding.'

She drew back, her look questioning him. 'Oh—why?'

'Because, my lovely girl, we must consider the proprieties,' he teased. 'We haven't the vestige of a chaperon in sight, and how *do* you suppose we can let our public suspect our morals have slipped?'

Danielle laughed. 'All right, banish me if you must. And I suppose I should thank my stars that if you hadn't needed a chaperone for the cruise, I shouldn't be here with you now?'

Cabot agreed, 'Mm, a neat move on my part. It got to you, didn't it?'

She shook him gently. 'I've told you—*none* of your ploys "got to" me. I grabbed at the job for those wretched reasons of my own. I only saw it as a means to my end of cutting you down to size—somehow, until Gina hinted you'd roped me in as cover for your affair with Louise. As chaperon to Louise, not for Gina, as you'd claimed. And then I was shocked to find I was jealous.'

'Good,' said Cabot smugly. 'I'd hoped to drive you to it. But Gina was way off beam. I pressganged you on board——'

'You did *not*!'

'I like a girl of spirit. To repeat—I engaged you and paid you for my own three-pronged purpose—to keep you under my eye, to keep other men at bay and to keep you committed to your word to me through *this*,' he touched the diamond on her finger 'until I did get through your guard as I knew I meant to. As I thought once I had, but I was mistaken.'

She turned her face into the hollow of his shoulder. 'You weren't mistaken,' she told him softly.

Cabot drew a long breath. 'Now she tells me!' he murmured in mock relief, and gathered her into eager, yearning arms again.

The hot afternoon sun of the Midi dazzled on the lawns and avenues of the Casino Gardens, and sparkled and dimpled on the sea. At a window heavily curtained in écru linen Danielle and her companion looked down at the lines of cars slowly circling in search of parking in front of the Hotel de Paris, before moving off round the avenues and returning to try again.

Gina, pressed into service as Danielle's bridesmaid, had already left for the church, leaving Danielle, who had been dressed early by her salon's fitter and *vendeuse*, to wait for the bridal car with Carlos Diego, who was to give her away.

The arrival of Carlos by air had been a surprise. Felipe and Louise were back in Lisbon now, enabling him to leave the estate at Cabot's urgent plea of Danielle's lacking a father or an uncle or even a close friend among the whole welter of strangers who would be there. Most of them without a hope of getting into the church, but not a man or woman jack among them who would admit to having missed the Cabot Steele wedding, Carlos told Danielle Cabot had said over the telephone. 'And it looks as if he were right,' Carlos said now of the milling cars. 'One has to hope that when the time comes, they will let *our* car through!'

'Yes. How long now?' Danielle asked.

'Any minute perhaps. Three or four at most.' Carlos stood back to appraise her gown, her hair, the graceful fall of her bouquet of orchids and white rosebuds. 'You make Cabot a lovely bride, but you kept us wondering when, for a very long time. It wasn't until Louise came home that she said the date was settled. I told her I'd have tried to be patient if she had wanted to wait over for it. But that wasn't quite true, I'm afraid,' he admitted. 'I was missing her a great deal, as I always do when we are apart.'

Lucky Louise to be so valued, and in a different way, lucky Carlos to have kept such faith, thought Danielle. She said quietly, 'I hope Cabot will still feel like that about me when we've been married a few years. Does Louise know?'

A momentary shadow crossed his kindly face and passed. 'It doesn't really matter, that,' he said simply. '*I* know all she means to me, and that's enough.' He glanced at his watch and then out of the window. 'There's your car. The usher is clearing the way for it to get to the steps. Come, give me your arm and we'll go down.'

And so Danielle came to Cabot, out of the sunshine into the shadows of the church, its dim interior fragrant with flower scents and, just where he stood awaiting her, shafted with coloured light from a transept window.

Outside there had been crowds of sightseers; cameras had clicked, photographers had pleaded for room. But she had been no more aware of them than she was of the rustle of admiration from the packed pews around her in this moment of coming to Cabot as his bride, when promise and hope and a total awareness of love leaped between them on a vital electric filament all their own.

She reached him. He stepped to meet her, his grave smile taking her to his heart. Slim and ethereal in a shimmer of creamy satin, she stood by his side to the height of his tall shoulder and made her vows to him; heard and trusted his to her.

No longer the pawn she believed he had callously made of her—now his wife . . . *his*.

Harlequin® Plus

A WORD ABOUT THE AUTHOR

Jane Arbor is one of Harlequin's veteran authors. Her first Romance, *City Nurse* (#423), was published in 1958. Eight years and many Romances later came the publication of *A Girl Named Smith,* which holds the distinction of being Harlequin's one thousandth title.

City Nurse, A Girl Named Smith and the book you are now holding were all written in the same "white-walled, black-beamed, Anne Hathaway-thatched cottage" north of the Thames River that has been Jane's home for more than thirty years. Here, wild pheasants freely roam the garden, and generations of beloved domestic animals have come and gone.

Before her marriage Jane Arbor owned a bookstore, and her experience there taught her that of all stories, romances provide the greatest amount of reading pleasure. Now, writing books that people want to read is a way of life for this hardworking author.

She writes every afternoon, seven days a week. If a book is "being difficult," she forces herself to leave it for a while. If, on the other hand, it is going well, "it would be rank cruelty to stay away."

When an idea for a new novel is germinating in her mind, Jane may first come up with either the background or the motivations of the characters. "If I begin with a well-researched background," she explains, "then sometimes it proves difficult to get the characters to play against it. In fact, once a colorful background waited five years before I used it in a novel!"

HARLEQUIN CLASSIC LIBRARY

Great old romance classics from our
early publishing lists.

FREE BONUS BOOK

On the following page is a coupon with which
you may order any or all of these titles. If you
order all nine, you will receive a FREE book—
Doctor Bill, a heartwarming classic romance
by Lucy Agnes Hancock.

The thirteenth set
of nine novels in the
HARLEQUIN CLASSIC LIBRARY

Great old favorites...
Harlequin Classic Library

Complete and mail this coupon today!

FREE BONUS BOOK

Harlequin Reader Service

U.S.A.
40 South Priest Drive
Tempe, AZ 85281

In Canada
649 Ontario Street
Stratford, Ontario N5A 6W2

Please send me the following novels from the Harlequin Classic Library. I am enclosing my check or money order for $1.50 for each novel ordered, plus 75¢ to cover postage and handling. If I order all nine titles at one time, I will receive a FREE book, *Doctor Bill*, by Lucy Agnes Hancock.

☐ 109	☐ 112	☐ 115
☐ 110	☐ 113	☐ 116
☐ 111	☐ 114	☐ 117

Number of novels checked @ $1.50 each =	$_____
N.Y. and Ariz. residents add appropriate sales tax	$_____
Postage and handling	$_____ .75
TOTAL	$_____

I enclose _____
(Please send check or money order. We cannot be responsible for cash sent through the mail.)
Prices subject to change without notice.

Name _____
(Please Print)

Address _____
(Apt. no.)

City _____

State/Prov. _____

Zip/Postal Code _____

Offer expires August 31, 1983   30556000000

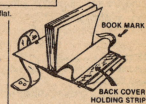